DEVIL'S SNARE

WENDY WANG

*Dedicated to the women who
supported me while I wrote this book.
Paula, Helen, Peggy, Gwen
and my mother in heaven, Carrie.
I love you all!*

CHAPTER 1

Two thoughts struck Charlie Payne when she entered the Kitchen Witch Café: the delicious aroma of her cousin Jen's fried chicken still made her mouth water, and there was a dead person hanging around.

A blast of cold air hit the back of her neck as soon as the jangling bell above the door announced her arrival but she didn't bother to look for an air vent. It was March. Too early for air conditioning, and the door had already closed behind her, blocking the damp, late morning air. This chill came from someone dead. She scanned the bustling restaurant, looking for the most obvious signs: dark shadows, half-torsos or full body apparitions that were just not quite solid. Unfortunately, it wasn't always easy to tell the living from the dead. A lot depended on

1

the dead person. How long they'd been dead. Whether they knew they were dead, or whether they simply wanted to hold onto this world.

Almost every table was filled with people dining on her cousin's country cooking. No one looked particularly dead. She took a deep breath and blinked slowly, waiting to feel the chill again. But it didn't come. Her shoulders relaxed, and she headed toward an empty space at the end of the lunch counter. A nearby diner's plate caught her eye. Two round grit cakes had been fried up like polenta, stacked and smothered in shrimp and gravy. Her stomach grumbled.

Charlie sat down on the fixed metal bar stool with red leatherette upholstery. A chalkboard stretched the length of the wall behind the lunch counter. The entire menu flanked a boxed section in the middle where her cousin wrote the daily specials.

A middle-aged man in a dark blue polo with a logo and khaki pants sat to her right. He pulled his wallet from his back pocket and laid two dollars down next to his now empty plate. His gold pinky ring winked at her, and he smiled at her before heading to the cash register to pay his bill.

An older gentleman with thin silver hair and a large liver spot on his forehead sat to her left. He wore a wrinkled and faded gray shirt with a navy sweater made worse for wear with moth holes in the sleeves. He held his hand up, waving at the young blue-haired waitress at the other end of the counter, but she didn't seem to see him. Charlie sighed. When was Jen finally going to see the light and fire that girl? She was the worst waitress Charlie had ever encountered.

The gentleman beside her finally gave up and leaned forward with his elbows on the counter. He folded his hands together. "Do you know what you're gonna get, young lady?"

Charlie perused the specials: fried chicken, shrimp and grit cakes and smothered sirloin steak. Each entrée came with two vegetables of the diner's choice and either a biscuit or cornbread.

"I do." Charlie called up a smile. "It's Wednesday. Fried chicken day. It's so good, it's won awards."

A soft smile stretched his lips and the thin crepe paper skin around his cloudy gray eyes wrinkled. He nodded. "Makes my mouth water just thinking about it."

"Mine too." Charlie glanced around, looking for her cousin. "The only thing that can hold a candle to it is the fish. On Fridays."

He bobbed his head up and down in agreement. "Oh yes. I do love fried fish. Do you know if it's fresh?"

"My cousin's the owner, and if she can't get it fresh, she doesn't serve it."

"Well, perhaps I'll have to come back on Friday. I'm not having much luck getting anything ordered today."

"I'm so sorry," Charlie said. "How long have you been waiting?"

"I'm not sure. A little while, I guess." He sighed. "My wife always served fish on Fridays."

"Well, it's a tradition."

"It is, indeed, which is exactly what we need these days." His gray eyes glassed over and his smile faded. "I haven't had fish since my wife passed away."

A cold finger touched Charlie's heart. Of course. It was the man's wife. She glanced over his shoulder to see if the woman's spirit would show herself.

"I'm so sorry for your loss," Charlie said. "How long ago did you lose her?"

"Oh, it's been a few months now." He sniffed and pressed his lips together, but she could still see them quivering. She closed her hands to keep herself from reaching out to touch him while silently scolding herself for holding back. Jen wouldn't have hesitated to give this man what he needed most—human contact. But Jen didn't see the things Charlie did. Some part of her didn't want the dead woman to be drawn out of this man just because she touched him and could see her. Spirits could deplete her energy, and some days she couldn't help it if they saw her first, but today wasn't one of those days.

He cleared his throat. "Well, thank you. I can say this with some certainty, young lady: If there's something you want to say to someone, don't hesitate. Because you never know when you won't be able to, you hear?"

"Yes, sir." Charlie nodded solemnly. "You should definitely come back on Friday. Have some fish in honor of your wife."

"I may just do that. Will you be here?"

"Probably." Charlie chuckled. "It all depends on if I have to work or not. I'm not on the schedule but sometimes I fill in when people call in sick."

He tapped his pinky on the counter. "What is it that you do?"

"I'm a call center representative for Bel-com."

"I like Bel-com. They're a good bank."

Technically, they were a credit union, but she didn't correct him. "I'm glad to hear you say that. They're a good company to work for."

"Indeed. I've got a safe-deposit box with them. Which reminds me, I need to make sure my daughter knows about it."

A warm hand touched the center of Charlie's back, making her look to her right. Deputy Jason Tate smiled and quirked one eyebrow. "Who are you talking to?"

Charlie raised her hand and pointed while turning her body to the man on her left. An icy hand wrapped around her heart and squeezed. The chair was empty. Charlie jumped to her feet and scanned the restaurant. Even if he had gotten up without her realizing it, he couldn't have reached the door so quickly that she wouldn't see him.

"Dammit," she muttered. "A dead man, I guess."

"What?" Jason took a step back, his expression morphing to panic.

"It's fine. He's gone."

Jason's gaze darted from her to the chair. "You sure?"

"Positive." Charlie took a seat at the counter again. She glanced around looking for the local busybodies who might gossip about crazy Charlie talking to herself. She didn't recognize most of the people in the restaurant, though. Many looked like tourists or snowbirds who were only here until the end of spring. "What are you doing here?"

Jason's body relaxed and he shrugged. "It's Wednesday,"

"Oh, right. Fried chicken," Charlie said.

"Hell, yeah." Jason rubbed his hands together and took a seat next to her. "So, what's your schedule like? You think you have some time to look at a file with me?"

"What kind of file?"

"Missing person."

"No, she does not," a feisty voice interrupted them.

Charlie and Jason both looked up at the same time to find Jen Holloway standing in front of them. Her tiny heart-shaped face reminded Charlie of a pixie. An angry, determined pixie from her expression. Jen was barely five feet tall but her fortitude and drive made her seem like a giant at times. "Whatever it is, Jason, you're just gonna have to do it without Charlie."

"Why? She just said—"

"I don't care what she just said. We have plans." Jen gave Charlie a pointed look. "You will just have to solve your case without her this time."

"I just wanted her opinion, that's all. Do you have time for an opinion?" he grumbled.

Charlie laughed. "Of course, I have time. We aren't leaving till Saturday."

"Early Saturday," Jen reminded.

"Where y'all goin'?" Jason asked.

Charlie smiled wide, but it was a false smile. Something to throw him off the trail should his detective senses go off. There was no need to tell him why they were taking a trip. The muscles in her face tightened. "To the mountains."

"You're going camping?"

The smug, dubious tone he used caused the hackles on Charlie's neck to rise, and she straightened her back. She kept her voice cool and controlled. "No, not this time. We've rented a cabin."

Jen folded her arms across her chest. She scowled and the lines in her forehead grew deep. "You think we don't camp?"

"I...I didn't say that." He held his hands up as if in surrender.

"Then what?" Jen challenged.

"It's just, y'all don't really strike me as outdoorsy. That's all." He shrugged one shoulder and all trace of the smirk disappeared.

"Oh, really?" Jen's mouth twisted into a sour bow. "I'll have you know that we are plenty outdoorsy. Not only do we fish and crab, but every single one of us can back a boat down a ramp."

Charlie sat back in her chair and crossed her arms to watch her cousin's tirade unfold. "And drive a boat."

"Right, and drive a boat."

"And throw a cast net." Charlie threw gas on her cousin's flaming retort.

Jen continued with her list, counting things off with her fingers. "And pitch a tent. And start a fire from sticks."

"Yep. We can't help that we're skilled *and* pretty," Charlie teased.

Jason snorted. His hazel eyes glittered as his lips twitched into a dry grin. "Even Daphne?"

Jen made a disgusted sound in her throat.

Charlie held up her palm as a stop sign. "Dude, Daphne can hold her own. If I had to choose one of us to be lost in the woods with, I'd choose Daphne. No offense, Jen."

"None taken." Jen waggled her head. "I'd pick her too."

Jason looked at both women like they were crazy and scratched his head. "I guess I'd have to see it to believe it."

"Oh, you'd believe it," Jen muttered. "And she'd be your first choice too."

"You know I just came in for fried chicken," Jason said, "not an argument."

"You know, I don't think I like your attitude," Jen said.

Charlie laughed and pointed at a sign on the wall that read: No shirt? No shoes? Bad attitude? No service!

"Um." Jason's face fell.

Charlie held her hand to her mouth and whispered loudly enough for her cousin to hear. "Maybe you should try apologizing."

"I'm sorry. Really. I'm sorry." Jason said the words so fast they sounded melded together. "Please don't make me leave. I've been thinking about your chicken all day."

"Fine. You're forgiven." Jen relaxed her shoulders and sighed. She tugged on the black apron she wore and pulled the order pad from the pocket. "Charlie, I know what you want. What about you, Jason? What're your veggies?"

"I'll have the fried okra and red ric,e please. And a biscuit and a glass of iced tea."

"Coming right up." Jen jotted it down and turned to

put the order in. Down at the other end of the counter, someone motioned for her and she headed that way.

Jason waited until Jen was out of earshot. "Man, your cousin's a spitfire. I thought she was the calm, nurturing one."

"You'd think that, wouldn't you? I sure wouldn't mess with her when she's mad."

"Good to know." Jason chuckled and shifted his gaze toward Jen.

Charlie watched him and shook her head. "I know what you're thinking."

Jason gave her a smug look. "Oh, really? What am I thinking?"

"You're thinking she's too small to be any real danger to anybody."

Jason's smug smile faded and morphed into a scowl. "I hate when you do that."

"What? Be right?" Charlie grinned.

"Shut up," he grumbled and fidgeted with the salt and pepper shakers in front of him.

Charlie laughed and looked him in the eye. "One day that doubt you call healthy skepticism is gonna bite you in the ass."

"Yeah? You see that with your third eye?" He air-quoted the last two words and smirked.

She cocked her head. "You know I can just take me

and my third eye home, right? Leave you to figure out your missing person case all on your own."

"Come on, don't be like that. I was just kiddin'." He put his shoulder against hers and leaned in, rocking against her.

"No, you weren't." There was no trace of teasing in her voice now. Jason's eyes widened at the accusation. She narrowed her eyes. Her tone still had a little bite to it. "You know, I am often amazed at your ability to dig in deep to your cognitive dissonance. It's like watching a pig wallow in mud then deny he's dirty."

He bristled. "You callin' me a pig?"

"If the snout fits."

His lips twisted with irritation, and he turned to face the counter. Charlie bit her lips together trying not to show her pleasure at getting under his skin.

"Okay, here you go," Jen said, putting two glasses of iced tea on the counter in front of them. Jen's gaze bounced between the two of them. "Everything okay?"

"Fine." Charlie picked up her glass and took a sip of the sweet amber-colored liquid. From the corner of her eye she saw Jason take a sip too. The tea cooled her mouth and throat, refreshing her mood, and immediately the tension she felt from her partner's slight washed away. Charlie glanced down at the glass and then up at her cousin. Jen didn't meet her gaze, but instead stared at Jason. What was she up to?

"Y'all make the best tea," Jason said. He took two more gulps and wiped his mouth with the back of his hand.

"I'm so glad to hear that." Jen smiled.

"I don't know what you put in it, but I always feel better after having your tea, Jen."

Jen's smile widened. "It's my own special brew. A trade secret."

Charlie pushed the glass away. It should've occurred to her before now that her cousin may have been using magic to make the drink so sought after. If someone came into the diner with a bad mood, all it took was a sip or two of Jen's sweet tea to make it dissipate.

"Well, it's downright addicting." He drained the glass.

Jen grabbed a pitcher from the counter behind them and refilled the drink, taking care to add some extra ice to the cup. She reached for Charlie's glass to top it off, but Charlie stopped her.

"No, thank you." Charlie gave her cousin an admonishing glare. She would make sure she questioned her about exactly what was in her secret brew.

Jen sniffed and turned her attention from her cousin. "So, Jason, how's your mama doing?"

"She's doing pretty good. The bed and breakfast will be open for business at the end of April, so she's busy planning that."

"That's great," Jen said. "I'm so glad that things

worked out for her." Jen referred to the very first case she worked on with Jason, ridding his mother's property of a troublesome ghost.

"So, y'all are leaving Saturday?" Jason asked.

"Early Saturday," Charlie reminded him.

"Is Evan going with you?"

"No, actually Evan is on spring break next week, and he's going on a trip with his dad to the Bahamas."

"And with his dad's new girlfriend," Jen added.

Charlie scowled and reached for the tea after all. She took a sip. Jen quirked her eyebrow and an I-told-you-so smile played at the corners of her mouth.

"Really?" Jason nodded, mild shock lacing his voice. "Interesting. I thought he was still hung up on you."

Charlie took a deep breath. "Nope. He's not. Which is good. It's better this way. He's happy."

"Whatever you say." Jason took a sip of tea.

Something about his dubious tone set her teeth on edge. Charlie's temper flared. "Do you want me to help you or not?"

Jason sat back in his chair and studied her for a minute. "You want me to run a background check on her? What's her name?"

"Heather. And, no. Of course not," Charlie said, sounding only half-appalled. "I've met her. I certainly wouldn't let my son just go off with anyone I didn't at least meet. Trust me, Scott will eventually get bored."

"Your Spidey senses tell you that?" Jason quipped.

"No, ten years of marriage did," she said.

"Well, you never know. Maybe good old Heather will work out."

Charlie picked up her tea glass and clinked it with his. "Here's hoping."

* * *

On Thursday morning, Charlie stopped at The Kitchen Witch to have a quick breakfast with Daphne and Lisa before her meeting with Jason. She spotted her cousins at a booth at the back.

"Are y'all early or am I late?" she said, pushing in next to Daphne.

"Neither." Lisa glanced up at the clock on the wall. "I'd say we're all right on time."

Daphne handed Charlie a menu and she opened it, pretending she would have time to order something.

"So," Charlie lowered her voice to a whisper, "any chance there's a spell that will make a day last thirty-six hours? I'm not going to get everything done for our trip."

Before anyone could answer, Jen appeared with a coffee pot. "Ha!" Jen poured refills for Lisa and Daphne, and a new cup for Charlie. "Now, that really would be magic."

"Are you gonna get a break?" Lisa took two sugar packs, tore them open and emptied them into her cup.

"Does it look like I'm gonna get a break?" Jen asked, waving the pot at her café full of customers. "Y'all will just have to do it without me. Darby called in sick."

Lisa cocked an eyebrow as she dabbed her finger in the crumbs of her muffin. "So you trust us to plan something as important as Charlie's initiation into our coven on our own?"

Jen gave the table a swipe with her towel, then tucked it back into the waistband of her apron. "Oh, I'll have final right of refusal before we take off for the weekend." She winked at Charlie then moved on to the next booth.

The week away in the mountains of North Carolina for some R&R was only the cover story. For months now, Charlie had been studying witchcraft under Evangeline. She'd already hesitated once at becoming part of the coven, but her cousins had all encouraged her to join them. It had been Lisa's idea to wait until Ostara, the witches' high holiday that coincided with the Vernal equinox. What better way to finally claim her birthright than to be initiated at the start of the season for rebirth? Charlie had kept the secret from everyone outside the circle of cousins for weeks now. There was no need to reveal the real reason for the trip to Jason and subject herself to his harassment.

"So," she said, dosing her coffee with milk and three packets of sugar, "what do you have for me?"

Lisa shoved a list of items across the table. "This is your shopping list and a few things you need to pack for the spirit circle. You'll find them around your house. Go over the list twice. You don't want to forget anything."

While Charlie studied the list, Daphne searched through her brown leather tote bag until she found a glossy covered travel book. Attached to it with a rubber band was a small thin book with an ominous black-and-white photo on the cover of a sign that read *Devil's Snare. Do not enter.*

"What's that?" Charlie asked.

Daphne held it up and displayed the cover. "Something I thought would be fun to check out. It's supposed to be about this place not too far from where we're staying. Evidently, it's supposedly an entrance to hell or something. The trees there are all dead, and people who go into the woods don't come out."

Charlie reached over and touched the book's cover. Her fingers twitched a little and her lip curled in disgust. "Why do you have it?"

Daphne shrugged one shoulder. "It looked interesting. I thought maybe the place was haunted, but it turns out the trees all died from some disease. Not because of the devil or a ghost. Only they didn't really

know that two hundred years ago when the legend was
born. They blamed it on local girl. Said she was a witch."

"Well, of course, they did," Lisa chimed in, wiping her
mouth with a paper napkin. "When in doubt…"

"A legend?" Charlie said.

"No way." Lisa's disgust played across her narrowed
eyes and downturned mouth.

"It could be fun," Daphne said, sounding like a little
girl.

"No. We are not going on a ghost hunt. This is too
important for Charlie."

Charlie drained her coffee cup and stuck her list in
her wallet, then checked her watch. "Well, I'm gonna let
y'all fight it out. I need to run. Thanks for this, Lisa. I'll be
like Santa. Check my list twice."

She turned to Daphne. "I wouldn't tell Jen about your
book. You know how she gets." On the way out, she
mulled over the selection of freshly baked muffins next to
the cash register.

CHAPTER 2

J ason's mind was lost in the contents of a blue
folder when Charlie walked into his office and
dropped a brown paper bag on his desk in front
of him. He gave her a long look and watched her
set down a tall to-go cup of iced tea next to it, and then
take a seat in the chair in front of his desk.

"What's this?" He opened the bag and stuck his nose
into it before she could answer. He breathed in the scents
of lemon, blueberry, and... was that lavender?

"Today's special."

Jason muttered to himself as he pulled the muffin
from the bag and peeled back the paper liner. He sunk
his teeth into it and moaned. "Oh, my God," he said with
his mouth full. "I don't know what she puts in these

things, but I swear to God they are the best thing I've ever tasted."

"I know," Charlie said. "You'd think they were made with magic or something."

Jason narrowed his eyes and his lips puckered as he thought hard about her last statement. He wasn't quite brave enough to come out and ask though. Did she really use magic in them? Charlie probably would have told him the truth, but some part of him didn't want to believe it, even if it was true.

"So, what do you have for me?" she asked.

Jason broke the muffin into smaller pieces. "It's just a case file I want you to look at. I don't want to give you too much information. Don't want to influence you."

Charlie nodded. "Yeah, that wouldn't help your case."

"Come on, let's go someplace quiet." Jason glanced across the busy office. His partner Marshall Beck gave him a nod, and a couple of the other deputies looked away conspicuously. Even after all these months, they still watched Charlie when she came into the office. They were skeptics, or maybe it was just jealousy. Since he'd met her, he'd closed more cases and found more solid evidence to back up his cases than all the others combined.

Charlie got up and followed him to one of the interview rooms. She sat down at the small wooden table across from the two-way mirror.

Jason sat across from her and set a manila folder down on the table. He took a notebook from the front pocket of his uniform.

Charlie laid her hand on top of the envelope. There was no questioning in her statement. "This is a cold case."

"Come on, you know the drill. Just give me your first impression from it. Whatever comes to mind." He poised his pen against the paper.

Charlie sighed. "That's my first impression. Is it wrong?"

"Um," Jason met her confused gaze. "No, it's not cold."

"You sure?"

"Yeah, pretty sure. I took the report myself."

"Fine." Charlie opened the folder and laid one hand down on the report in front of her. Inside the folder behind the report was a photograph of a teen boy. He wasn't that much older than Evan, maybe fifteen, and a pang of sadness filled Charlie's heart when she touched the photo. Inexplicably, her eyes clouded with tears and she sniffed.

Jason hated to see any woman cry, but it especially hit him hard when it was Charlie. She felt so much sometimes, he didn't know how she could stand it. He reached across the table and put his hand on top of hers. "You okay?"

Charlie cleared her throat and pulled her hand from beneath his. Quickly, she swiped at her eyes. "Yeah, I'm

fine. He's not dead, if that's what you're worried about."
She touched the picture, tracing her finger over the boy's
face. "Wow, so many emotions. He's so angry. And sad.
And scared." She looked up into Jason's face. Her blue
eyes were still glassy. "He's been abandoned. That's what
this feels like. As if nobody in the world cares about him."
Charlie touched her hand to her heart and a sob escaped
her.

Panic fluttered in his chest as he watched her weep
into her hands. "We can stop. You don't have to do this."

"No. It's okay. Really." She breathed in and out
through her nose and closed her eyes until, little-by-little,
she got herself under control. "I see him running
alongside a train. It's night and there's no moon. He
wasn't sure he could catch the train and pull himself onto
it, but he did. He climbed all the way to the top of the
boxcar. He laid down and stared up at the sky full of stars.
And kept thinking, 'I'm free.'" Charlie swallowed hard.
"He ran away from something oppressive. Or someone."

"His foster father. Evidently the guy's a real asshole,"
Jason said. Charlie's eyes filled with questioning. "Or so
the social worker says."

Charlie nodded and blew out a breath. She closed her
eyes and swayed back and forth so slightly that most
people wouldn't notice. But Jason had seen her do this
before, and he knew what came next. He put his pen to
paper again and waited.

"I see the letters C&R on the box cars. He jumped on the train and rode it out of the area."

"Any idea when this happened?"

Charlie glanced down at the missing person's report. "It says March thirteenth." She frowned. "But that doesn't seem right, based on the cycle of the moon."

"What do you mean?"

"I mean the moon was full on the twelfth of March. This says he took off three days before that. So, it would've been really bright in the sky. He also didn't have on a jacket or anything, so it wasn't cold." She took her phone from her purse and typed something into it. "Yeah, weatherdog.com says the temps were in the forties when he disappeared. Even Evan would put on a jacket at night and he's a furnace."

Jason nodded and wrote it down. "How do you know all that about the moon cycles?"

Charlie shrugged. Her gaze fell on the mirror behind him. "It's just something Evangeline's been teaching me."

"Why?" He cringed at the judgment in his voice when she bristled at the question. "I mean are you studying astronomy or something?"

"Something," Charlie said coolly. "Does it matter?"

"No, I was just curious, that's all. Anyway, the social worker figured she was lying."

"Who?" Charlie asked.

"The foster mother. The social worker stopped by

unexpectedly, and the foster mother told her he'd been gone a couple of days, but she thought it might be longer."

"Why would she wait so long?"

"My guess is that she wanted to continue getting her payment from the state. It was actually the social worker who reported him missing."

"That's awful," Charlie said. "Where are his parents?"

"The mother's dead. Drank herself to death, from what the social worker said. The father was never in the picture. He died when the boy was a baby."

"Oh, my god, that's so sad. How long's he been in the system?"

"Since he was five."

Charlie looked back at the picture. "When he left, all he could think was that he was free."

"Well, that's not heartbreaking at all, is it?" Jason said, his voice full of irony. "Truth is, he may be free for now, but there are plenty of people out there who'll take advantage of him."

"What can we do?"

"Not much I can do, especially if he left the area. No chance you could tell me which direction he went in, is there?"

Charlie glanced down at the picture again, then closed her eyes. Lines of concentration carved her forehead and her jaw tightened. After a minute of holding her breath, she blew it out and opened her eyes. "Sorry." She shook her head. "I got nothing. Maybe you could call the company and find out what their nighttime schedules are and where they go."

Jason shrugged. "Yeah. It's worth a try. Thank you for coming. I really appreciate your help and the muffin."

"I don't feel like I really did anything for you."

"Of course, you did. I didn't have a lead, and now I do."

"Well, I just hope something pans out. Can you tell me what his name is?"

"What? You don't know?" Jason teased. Charlie gave him a death stare, and he laughed. "Sorry." He pointed to the place on the form with the missing person's name.

Charlie looked down at Jason's finger and read Jamison Goforth.

She frowned. "Hmmm."

"What?"

"That's not right. That's not his name."

"Well, that's what the social worker gave me."

"I understand, but I'm telling you, that's not his name."

"Charlie, I don't know what to say. That's the name that was given to me."

"I keep hearing DJ. DJ."

"Well, maybe the kid liked to mix music. Or maybe it was a nickname."

"Maybe." Charlie sighed softly and touched her finger to the boy's name on the form. Her expression softened and her eyes became distant, as if she were looking at something far away.

"What do you see?" Jason prompted.

"I see a pretty young woman with long dark hair holding a baby in her arms, rocking him back and forth. I can't see her face because of her hair, but she's nuzzling him and calling him DJ. I love you, DJ. Mama loves you." Her voice rose, sounding almost like a little girl's. Jason's forearms broke into goose bumps as he listened to her slip into the head of the girl in her vision. "I love you, DJ. I love you so much."

Charlie's face jerked up and tears streaked her face now. "No, please. Just one more minute with him. Please."

Charlie closed her eyes and her shoulders shook. She held her arms as if she were holding a baby and nuzzled against the invisible child. "Never forget me. Okay? I will never forget you." Charlie acted as if she were giving the baby to someone else and then wept into her hands. It took her a few minutes to get herself under control. Jason watched her, waiting for any sign that Charlie had returned. Finally, she looked up at him and looked him straight in the face. "Was the boy adopted?"

"I don't—" Jason shook his head. "I have no idea. Is that even relevant?"

"Maybe." She wiped the tears from her cheek. "Maybe

he found out. Maybe he went looking for her. For his birth mother. She felt young."

"How young?"

"Eighteen, maybe nineteen. And alone."

Jason scribbled the info onto his notepad. "We'll see where it leads."

"Evan has a friend who was adopted. This kid has everything. Two adoring parents, every toy imaginable, good school. But he is always still thinking about his birth mother. He didn't want to go live with her; he just wanted to know things about her. Maybe it was the same for DJ. Especially since his parents were out of the picture and he was in foster care."

"Did you see that too?"

"No. Just a theory."

"Well, it's a good theory, I guess, if he knew he was adopted. Anything else?"

"That's all I got."

"Well, thank you. I appreciate it. I'll walk you out."

Jason closed the manila folder and tucked it under his arm. He dropped it off on his desk before leading Charlie out of the building.

"So." Charlie gave him a sly smile. "You and the social worker, huh?"

Jason's eyes widened. He stopped in the middle of the lobby and stared at her. "What are you talking about?"

"Come on. You don't usually investigate runaways. I

mean, not beyond the cursory report. You either like her or you're dating her."

A choked sound escaped his throat, and he gaped at her for a good thirty seconds. The image of Shelby Banting flashed through his mind. He had flirted with her when she'd asked him for a favor. Her red lips had parted, and she'd pushed her dark hair behind one ear, revealing her long, sexy neck. He scowled. "Dammit, you can be annoying sometimes."

Charlie laughed, not the least bit offended. "That's what they tell me."

"I am *not* dating her. She's just a friend."

"Uh-huh. I'm sure she is."

He hated the smugness in her voice. There was no use lying to her, though. He'd had to learn that lesson a few times before it finally sank in. He glanced around to see who might be listening then leaned in close. "I'm just helping her out. That's all. She kind of screwed this up. Missed a couple of appointments with the foster parents. She feels guilty that the boy went missing on her watch."

"Oh." Charlie nodded, a smirk still on her lips. Something in her tone made him think she didn't believe him. "Sure."

"We're not dating." Jason cringed at the crescendo of his voice. "She's not my type."

Charlie's smug smile faded, and she shifted her feet. His heart sank. He'd said too much. A quick glance into her face told him all he needed to know about her thoughts on the matter. Awkwardness crept up between them. He blew out a heavy breath. Was she still hung up on that mortician? He wasn't sure, but it apparently didn't matter. "Anyway, I need to get back upstairs."

"Right," she said and started to turn toward the exit.

"Hey," he called after her. "How long will you be gone?"

"A week."

"Well, have fun."

She smiled, and the easiness between them returned. "Thanks, I will."

"Text me when you get back."

"I will."

He started for the stairs but a cold finger of intuition touched his heart, stopping him in his tracks. He turned to tell her to be careful. But it was too late. She was gone.

CHAPTER 3

Friday morning, Charlie stopped at the Kitchen Witch Café to have breakfast before running the long list of errands her cousin had given her. The restaurant bustled with diners, so she took one of the free seats at the counter. She inhaled the heavenly scent of banana pancakes and bacon lingering in the air. Her mouth watered as she gave the specials on the chalkboard a cursory glance. She already knew what she wanted, and she watched Jen at the other end of the counter making bright chitchat while filling coffee cups as she went. When she stopped in front of Charlie, she grabbed a white cup from beneath the counter and set it in front of her. Jen filled it three quarters of the way up then put a small stainless steel pitcher full of milk on the counter. Charlie topped off the cup with milk, filling it to the brim before ripping open three packets of sugar. She stirred her sweet concoction and took a sip, closing her eyes as the warm liquid slipped down her throat.

"Nectar of the gods," she muttered and opened her eyes.

Jen laughed and took her order pad from the front pocket of her apron. "Banana pancakes with maple pecan syrup and bacon coming right up."

"And they call me a mindreader," Charlie teased.

"Nope," her cousin quipped, giving her a knowing grin. "You're just very predictable. Especially when it comes to your food."

Charlie shrugged. "Well, a girl's gotta have some sort of stability in her life."

"You keep telling yourself that," Jen teased and headed for the pass-through to put in the order.

Charlie wrapped her hands around her warm cup. She took another sip and breathed in the scent of the fresh coffee.

The door opened and the bell above it rang announcing another patron. The hairs on the back of her neck stood at attention and her heart fluttered against her will. She didn't have turn around to find the cause. She knew just by his energy that Tom Sharon had stepped into the café. Charlie raised her gaze, staring straight ahead.

She felt him stop and hesitate. Was he wondering

what move he should make? Whether he should just turn around and leave or take the empty seat at the end of the counter and pretend he didn't see her? Either of these two options would have been fine with her.

"Good morning, Charlie," she heard him say. Damn. He went a different way.

"Good morning," she said, trying not to sound too cool but also not too inviting. After all, she had an empty seat next to her. She didn't want him to get it in his head that it was okay for him to sit there.

Tom sat next to her and leaned with his elbows on the counter.

Charlie glanced at him and forced a smile to be polite. His handsome face caught her off guard, causing her stomach to flip flop. Damn him and his glamour.

"Hi," he said in a soft, silky voice.

"Hi." Of course, he took the seat next to her. Of course, he did. Charlie looked at the two empty seats near the end of the counter then glanced at the empty two-top table near the front window. She sighed and shifted her gaze to her coffee cup.

"I haven't seen you in a while." He took a napkin from the chrome holder in front of him and started to shred it. "How've you been?"

"Good," she said.

"How's Evan?"

"Good."

An awkward silence settled between them. Charlie shifted this way and that but couldn't get comfortable, then finished off the rest of her coffee. She glanced toward her cousin who was chatting with a customer at the opposite end of the lunch counter.

"Jen looks good."

"Uh-huh." Charlie nodded.

Tom blew out a heavy breath and from the corner of her eye she saw his shoulders slump in defeat. "Is it always going to be like this?"

"Like what?" Her words sounded too shrill in her ears and she cringed.

He shrugged one shoulder. "Strained conversation made up mostly of me asking questions and you offering up one-word responses."

"It's not that bad. Don't be dramatic."

"You sound angry."

Charlie bristled. "Well, I'm not."

"Do you want me to move?" he asked softly.

Some part of her screamed, *Yes, dammit, yes. Go sit in the corner out of my sight.* But another part of her, a part she didn't quite want to acknowledge, piped up. "It's a free country. You can sit wherever you want."

"Hi, Tom." Jen pulled a white coffee cup from beneath the counter. "Coffee or hot tea today?"

"Hot tea would be lovely. Thank you."

Jen nodded and smiled, then gave Charlie a pointed

look. *Be nice,* her cousin's eyes told her. Charlie twisted her lips into a defiant scowl. "Coming right up." Jen headed to the coffee station and filled a small metal pitcher with hot water. She grabbed two tea bags and placed them on a saucer. A few seconds later, she put the pitcher and tea bags in front of Tom. "So, how are things at the mortuary?"

"Things are good," he said in a solemn voice. "Death will always be in business."

Jen nodded. "Indeed, it will." She pulled her order pad from her front apron pocket and poised her pen. "So, what are you gonna have today?"

Charlie stared at her cousin, her mouth ajar. How could she treat him like he was just like anyone else? He was a reaper, wearing a human face. He didn't need to eat.

"I am betting that Charlie ordered the banana pancakes." Tom's mouth drew up into a sly smile.

"You would win that bet." Jen winked at Charlie.

"I'll have the same." He tore open a packet of sugar and poured it into his tea.

"You won't be sorry." Jen scribbled the order on her pad.

"May I?" Tom pointed to the half-full pitcher of milk in front of Charlie.

"Of course." She pushed it over to him.

"So, it's spring break soon?"

"Yes." Charlie twirled her finger around the rim of her cup and glanced down the counter at her cousin. Jen stopped to fill another coffee cup.

"Are you doing anything special with Evan?"

Charlie didn't look at him. "Evan's spending spring break with his dad."

"Well, that will be nice for him. Are *you* doing anything special?"

She hesitated. Should she tell him? Part of her hated that he was a lying liar and that she couldn't trust him. But another part of her missed their easy banter. Missed that she could truly be herself with him, without judgment.

"My cousins and I are heading to the mountains of North Carolina for the week," Charlie answered after a moment.

"That sounds wonderful." His tone seemed a little wistful.

She straightened her back. Not wanting her moment of softness to give him the wrong impression. It didn't matter if she missed him. He was not human, no matter what sort of mask he presented to the world and there was nothing that would change that fact. "I'm still mad at you," she blurted out and then cringed inwardly. *Way to go, Charlie.*

"You have every right to be."

"What you did was inexcusable." She fiddled with the spoon next to her cup, turning it over.

"I know," he said in a small voice. "But is it unforgivable?"

She met his gaze and was drawn into his brown eyes. Fiery amber flecks made her heart melt just a little. "I don't know."

"I don't expect things to be the way they were before."

Why was her life always broken into before and after? It seemed things were before she married Scott and after she divorced Scott. Now, it was Tom stepping into those shoes. Before she learned his identity and after.

"Some things can't be unlearned or unseen. Or undone," she said.

"You're right." He took a sip of his tea and flipped the spoon over, laying it across the cup. "I understand." He rose from his seat, took a fancy black leather wallet from his back pocket and pulled out a five-dollar-bill. He laid the money next to the cup of tea and glanced up to catch Jen's attention. She smiled and headed back his way. "Can I get my pancakes to go please?"

"Of course. Is everything okay?" Jen called up a surprised smile. Jen's gaze bounced between Charlie and back to Tom.

"Everything is perfect," he said in a silky, charming voice. "I just realized I need to get into work early. You know the dead don't wait."

"Right." Jen's face grew taut as her smile widened. "I'm sure Charlie completely understands that. Don't you, Charlie?"

Charlie nodded, giving her cousin a dirty look. "Of course. Who better to understand than me?"

"It'll just be a few minutes," Jen said. "You want some more tea while you wait?"

"No, thanks. I'm going to go grab a paper outside."

"Sure. No problem. It's good to see you."

"You too. Have a great vacation if I don't see you for lunch."

"Thanks." Jen smiled and something silent passed between them. Charlie perked up, watching the exchange.

"See you around, Charlie." Tom turned and walked away before Charlie could respond.

Jen's lips deflated into a flat line and Charlie braced herself.

"Okay." Jen leaned in close and lowered her voice, but it didn't diminish the anger flaring beneath. "It's been almost five months. I'm not saying that you should date him. I mean, after all, he is—well—what he is. But he saved your life. And that means something. Maybe you should cut him some slack," her cousin said through partially gritted teeth.

"He betrayed me," Charlie hissed and glanced around

to see if anyone was even noticing their little back-and-forth exchange.

"So did Scott but you don't have any problem forgiving him." Her cousin's rebuke hit her hard, sending a shard of pain through her heart.

"That's different. Scott's the father of my child."

"Yes, and for years he was an abusive asshole," Jen whisper-yelled.

"He never hit me," Charlie countered.

"No, he didn't raise a finger. All he did was make you feel like nothing for nearly ten years." Jen's gaze bore into Charlie.

Charlie didn't dare look away. She narrowed her eyes and lowered her voice to a whisper. "I watched Tom die. Okay? When he didn't even have to. Do you have any idea how horrible that was?"

"Of course, I do. I was there, remember?" Jen's tone softened. "But he sacrificed his mortal form to save you. Not to hurt you. You think he didn't know the risk of showing you his real identity?"

"You know, if I didn't know better," Charlie said, her voice full of warning. "I'd think that you've been colluding with the enemy."

"He is not our enemy, and no matter what you think, he still cares about you. A lot."

Charlie scowled. "I don't want to forgive him. Not yet. Maybe not ever."

"I can't make you do anything you don't want to do." Jen straightened her spine and sniffed. "But I'm not above trying to guilt you into it."

"Noted. And I already knew that. If you think I forgot Brian McAfee, you've got another think coming," Charlie said trying to lighten things between them again.

"Oh, my god. That was fifteen years ago. Let it go already. Let it go." Her cousin sang the last line holding up her arms in a dramatic fashion. Charlie laughed. And just like that, things were healed between them. For a brief second, Charlie wondered if her cousin had employed a silent spell, but she pushed that thought away. Any other witch and it might have been a possibility, but her cousin didn't like to use magic on her family, regardless of any threats she might make.

On Friday afternoon, Charlie pulled her blue Honda Accord into Scott's driveway. She sighed and looked up at the big house she once shared with her ex-husband. Things had been better between them since last year when he almost died, but dread still weighed on her heart every time he asked her to come inside.

"You okay, Mom?" Her eleven-year-old son sat in the front seat next to her, his black backpack on his lap. He looked at her with his thoughtful blue eyes. One of the few things he inherited from her. She cupped his cheek and called up a smile.

"Of course," she said. "Get your stuff out of the trunk, okay?" She reached down and lifted the trunk release. Evan hopped out and disappeared behind the trunk's door. She stepped out of the car and watched him wrangle the backpack and the black carry-on he'd asked to borrow. When she had asked what was wrong with the suitcase he had at his dad's house, Evan had told her, "It has a Captain America shield on it, Mom. And it's bright red. It's something a baby would carry." A bittersweet pang had filled her chest. It was only a couple years ago that he had loved that Captain America suitcase.

Charlie followed Evan toward the front porch. He stopped midway along the cement walkway. "You know you don't have to walk me to the door. I'm not a baby anymore."

"I know that," Charlie quipped. "But your dad asked to talk to me about something."

"Oh." He frowned. "You sure it's not 'cause you want to check out his plans?"

"I'm sure. But just so you know, you're still my son and your safety and well-being will always be my priority." She went to ruffle his hair, but he ducked her. She followed him inside and met Scott in the foyer.

"Charlie," Scott said, sounding entirely too happy to see her. "Thanks for coming in."

"You're welcome." She gave him a wary smile and waited for stern, unhappy Scott to appear.

"I know you're busy, what with Friday night dinner and all."

"It's fine, I wanted to make sure you had my information too."

"Great," Scott said.

Charlie opened her purse and pulled out a piece of paper with neatly typed rows of phone numbers for her cousins as well as emergency numbers for her uncle and aunt.

"Do you have anything similar for me?" she asked sweetly.

He looked over the list of names and numbers. "I didn't realize this was what you wanted. Why don't we go back to my office and I'll write down the numbers for you? I have something important I want to talk to you about."

"Sure." Dread coiled in her stomach. She'd hoped to avoid his office. Even as things had gotten better between them over the last few months, his office still made her feel a little like a child being pulled in to see the principal.

She followed him through the house, noting the changes to the living room since the last time she had been here. All the fussy cream and gold furniture and knickknacks that had furnished the living room were now gone. The walls had been painted a fresh pale gray and the new white couch and two modern-styled armchairs finished off the conversation area.

Charlie stopped to admire the new set up. She brushed her hand across the top of one of the chairs. The soft navy fabric tickled her palm. "You got new furniture."

"I know! It's great, isn't it?" Scott beamed. It'd been years since she had seen that much light in his face. "Heather thought we needed a change in here."

"Wow." She glanced around. "Heather has good taste."

"She does," he said, the admiration shining through his voice. "She's an interior designer, though, so it's sort of her thing."

"Of course," Charlie muttered. "Well, it certainly feels better in here."

"It does," he said. "Sometimes, I just like to come in here and sit now."

"I think that's great, Scott. I'm glad you're happy."

His eyes crinkled a little but something about his smile, which widened, made her wistful. She had loved him once, and he had loved her. But never in the fourteen years of knowing him had he ever smiled that way for her. "Thank you, Charlie. That means..." He nodded, and the lines deepened in his brow. "...a lot. I hope one day you'll be this happy again too."

Another bittersweet pang plucked at her heart. No

point in feeling regret now. She smiled. "So, you wanted to talk to me about something?"

"Right, come on. It's something I want to give you. For your trip."

"Okay." She followed him on through the living room and kitchen, down a short hallway to his office. They passed through the heavy walnut door and Scott crossed to his desk in four easy steps.

"Why don't you have a seat?" He pointed to the couch along the far wall. Charlie took a seat on the long leather Chesterfield sofa. Scott sat down next to her but not too close. He handed her a small white box. Her heart leapt into her throat. It looked like a jewelry box. "I want you to have this."

Charlie took it and hesitated opening it. Her cheeks flushed with heat. Why was she so nervous suddenly? Her voice shook a little. "What is it?"

"Just open it. It won't bite you."

"It's not jewelry, is it?"

"Charlie, you didn't even wear the jewelry I bought you when we were married. Why would I buy you jewelry now?" he said, sounding a little irritated.

"Good point." She relaxed her shoulders and lifted the lid off the box. She stared down at the contents of the box. Bewildered. "It's a knife?"

"Not exactly. It's a combination tool."

"Like a Swiss Army knife?" She took the tool from the

box and felt the weight of it in her hand. The cool metal gave off a pleasant energy, and she bit the inside of her cheek to keep from smiling. Just a few months ago she'd barely even noticed metal, much less the energy it gave off.

"Even better. See, the handle opens and it's pliers but it's also a cutter. See the little blade here. Very useful for cutting wire or twine."

"Okay," she said, watching him as he carefully fanned out tools from each of the handles.

"See, it's like a tiny tool set. Screwdriver, Phillips head screwdriver. Two different sized blades. Both of those are very sharp by the way, so be careful. A saw, a can opener. And then there's a place for a carabiner." He pulled something from his pocket and put it in her hand.

She stared down at the round antique brass object attached to a black carabiner. "Your compass."

"Yes." Scott nodded.

"Scott, I can't take your compass. Your grandfather gave you this." She pushed it back toward him, and he grabbed hold of her hand and closed her fingers around it.

"I want you to take it, Charlie. You can give it back to me after your trip if you like."

"Why?" Charlie met his steady gaze.

"Because you're going into the woods," Scott said matter-of-factly. "Evan said that you're going camping."

"We've rented a cabin. A pretty luxurious cabin, actually. We're not going camping in the backwoods. Trust me." She chuckled and tried to pull her hand out of his but his grip tightened. Her stomach fluttered with panic.

"Please?" He lowered his voice. "It'll make me feel better."

"Why?"

"I just want you safe. And to know that no matter what, you'll come back."

"Scott."

"Humor me. I'll never know if you don't pack it, but it will make me feel better knowing you have it."

Charlie sighed. She thought about arguing with him. Accusing him of trying to control her. Trying to find a way back into her life. But something inside her didn't think that was what was really going on. She gave him a weary smile. "Can I please have my hand back now?"

"Of course. Sorry." He let her go and glanced away. His cheeks filled with color.

She tucked the box with the tool and the compass into her bag. "Now are you gonna write down those numbers for me or what?"

"Yes, of course. I'll do that right now."

CHAPTER 4

The tires screeched against the asphalt. Charlie's head bounced hard against the headrest in the front passenger seat of Daphne's SUV. Out of instinct she grabbed for the bar above the window and held on for dear life. When the SUV finally came to a stop, they were too close to the car in front of them for Charlie's comfort. All three lanes of traffic stood still. Daphne's hands gripped the steering wheel, her knuckles white. She made a strangled gurgling laugh in the back of her throat.

"Jesus, Daphne!" Lisa yelled from the backseat. "What the hell?"

Daphne's gaze shifted to the rear-view mirror, and she scowled. "Sorry. Everything just stopped really fast."

"You okay, honey?" Charlie ignored Lisa and put her

hand on Daphne's shoulder. Her cousin was trembling a little.

"Yeah, I'm fine," Daphne muttered. "I really am sorry."

"It's okay, sweetie." Jen sat up and stretched. "Can you see what's going on?"

Daphne craned her neck. "Looks like construction. May as well get comfortable."

"Ugh." Lisa punched at the pillow she'd been leaning on and rearranged it so it was between her head and the window. "Wake me when we get there."

Charlie leaned over to find her bag with her spell notes and came up with Daphne's brown tote instead. Daphne grabbed it from her and her travel book fell out.

"I thought you were gonna get rid of that," Charlie said. She recognized the cover with the Devil's Snare photo.

"What is that?" Jen leaned forward and snatched the book out of Daphne's hand.

"Nothing," Daphne said, too innocently for anyone to believe.

"Why don't you tell Jen about it?" Charlie asked. Daphne shot her a look that could kill. Charlie smirked and shifted her gaze to Jen. "You see what you missed out on? Daphne had plans for a little adventure during our trip. We heard all about it the other morning. I'm sure Daphne would be happy to fill you in."

Daphne had a defensive tone when she explained the

story of Devil's Snare. When she finished she shrugged. "I just thought it would be interesting."

"No, you thought you'd end up with more videos for your YouTube channel," Lisa chimed in.

Daphne said sharply, "I thought you were sleeping."

"Who can sleep with y'all yammering away?" Lisa shifted in the backseat.

"It could still be fun to investigate. I mean the book still doesn't explain why hikers that venture in don't come out," Daphne argued.

Charlie thought of the box in her purse holding the compass that belonged to Scott. "It's really easy to lose your sense of direction in the woods. Especially if they're unfamiliar to you."

Jen thumbed through the book. Her fingers stopped on the photo of a painting of a young woman. Her fine features were set off by her dark hair and dark eyes. A slight smile curved her lips as if she held a secret. "Is this her?"

"Yeah. Abigail Heard. Eventually, she confessed to witchcraft," Daphne said.

"Probably after they tortured her," Lisa grumbled. "Sons of bitches."

Daphne pivoted her body so she could look at her cousins. "Supposedly she cursed the town right before they killed her."

"What kind of curse?" Jen continued to leaf through

the pages.

Daphne shook her head. "Oh, you know, nothing specific that I could tell from the book. The big thing is that people who go into the woods get lost and don't come out."

Lisa chuckled. "Well, that's kind of a dumb legend."

"I thought it was kind of interesting. We're not that far. Maybe we could check it out. You know, as part of Charlie's initiation." A chorus of no's came from her three cousins, and Daphne crossed her arms. "It was just an idea. That's all. Geez."

"Well, I'm still not sure what sort of witch I'm gonna make," Charlie said.

"You're gonna make a fine witch," Jen said.

"Yeah, and it's too late to back out now," Daphne chimed in. "Ostara is Monday. We're doing this. Even if we have to drag you kicking and screaming."

"Don't listen to her, Charlie," Lisa said. "If you don't want to be a witch, you don't have to be a witch. I don't know if anybody has actually said that out loud to you, but it's really all your decision. And nobody should be making you do it if you don't want to."

"It's not that I don't want to. I love the idea of being more like y'all, but—" Charlie shifted in her seat so she could turn and look at Lisa. She sighed. "I've failed almost every spell Evangeline has taught me in the last five months."

"Oh," Daphne said. "Well, that's totally normal. Didn't mama tell you that?"

"I...no." Charlie's cheeks filled with heat.

"It's not even a question of whether you're a witch or not. You have Payne blood running through your veins, just like all of us," Daphne said. "Own it."

"She still has a choice, Daphne. Not everybody wants to live this life. Once you go through vivification, there's no turning back. You can't turn the magic off like a light switch."

"Don't be afraid of turning on the switch, Charlie," Daphne said.

"No," Jen said. "Lisa's right. It's her choice. But you should know that failing at spells is part of the process. Even with magic in our veins, we all vivified at different times."

"That's true. Jen could do magic long before I could, even though I'm older," Lisa said. "Maybe you're just putting too much pressure on yourself to get it right. Whatever that means. And how do you know the spells didn't work?"

"Well, they were pretty straightforward spells. Stuff even a six-year-old witch could do," Charlie said. Her baby cousin Ruby had picked up the spell Evangeline tried teaching her with ease.

"You can't go by Ruby," Jen said. "She vivified as a baby. Just because Ruby can do a spell and you can't doesn't mean that you aren't a witch. Spells just may not be your thing."

"That's very true," Lisa chimed in. "I certainly can't see the dead."

"Right," Daphne said. "I make a mean potion and cast a glamour like it's nobody's business, but I can't do a locater spell half as well as Lisa."

"That's true," Lisa said.

"The point is we all have different gifts and magical abilities, but it doesn't make us any less a witch." Jen leaned forward and leveled her gaze on Charlie. "Trust yourself. And, of course, we're here to help."

"Absolutely," Lisa added.

"Anyway," Daphne said, "there are supposed to be these really gorgeous waterfalls near the forest in that book. I marked the pages in the travel book with the trail to get to them."

"Cool. We should go see them," Charlie said.

"We'll take a picture of the four of us. Start our own adventure wall," Lisa said.

"Now, that's an idea I can get behind," Charlie said.

"Yeah, and the cabin we're staying at really isn't that far," Daphne said. "I think we could actually hike to the waterfalls from it."

"These woods are that close to the cabin?" Lisa asked.

"Yep. But don't worry. It's just a stupid legend," Daphne said.

"Yes, somehow that doesn't really make me feel better," Lisa said. "Hand me that book please."

Jen passed the book to Lisa. A few strands of Lisa's long strawberry blond hair had come loose from the braid that slipped over one shoulder. The wisps fell softly around her face. She shared her sister's pixie-like features and her nose scrunched up as she flipped the book over and read the back of it.

"Well," Lisa said, thumbing through the pages to the several illustrations in the middle, "it does look like a big old tangle of woods. I bet that's why they can't find anybody. I mean, look at this." Lisa opened the book to a page showing an aerial view in winter. The gray branches crisscrossed each other like a cage.

"Hikers go in, but they don't come out," Charlie said.

"Well, we'll just steer clear, then." Jen grabbed the book from Lisa's hands and tucked it inside the backpack at her feet.

"Hey!" Lisa protested.

"You can read this later," Jen said. "This trip is supposed to be spiritual. Not full of negativity."

"Come on, it's just a ghost story about a witch," Lisa chided. "It's probably something that the locals made up to get people to come to their little Podunk town."

"Well, there's truth in all legends," Daphne said, sounding defensive. "And we all know that ghost stories can be real."

They all became quiet for a moment and the air grew heavy.

"Hey, traffic's moving." Lisa pointed toward the front windshield.

"Great. I don't know about y'all, but I'm hungry," Daphne finally said, breaking the heaviness. She inched the SUV forward. "Maybe we can stop for lunch at the next exit."

"It's only 10:30," Lisa said, looking at the expensive gold watch on her wrist.

"Okay, breakfast, then." Daphne argued.

"I'm with Daphne," Charlie said. "All I've had is coffee."

"I could eat," Jen said.

"All right, let's eat, then." Lisa folded up her pillow, shoving it between her head and the window. She closed her eyes. "Wake me when we get there."

CHARLIE DROVE DAPHNE'S FORD EXPLORER UP THE STEEP gravel driveway because she had the most experience using four-wheel drive. Daphne's round face pinched with panic and she held tight to the oh-shit-bar above her door. The others breathed an overdue sigh of relief once Charlie made it to the top and pulled into the large parking area to the side of the little cabin they'd rented.

Charlie pulled alongside an ancient Jeep Cherokee already parked there. Daphne had called the rental company, and the woman had agreed to give them the key early.

An older woman dressed in tan pants and a thick flannel buffalo plaid shirt over a T-shirt waved at them from the top step of the wide front porch. Daphne hopped out of the truck and headed up the steps.

Daphne greeted the woman. "Hi, Marion. Thank you so much for meeting us."

Marion smiled. "My pleasure." A few moments later, Charlie, Jen and Lisa joined Daphne on the steps. "I went ahead and got everything turned on and pulled all the covers from the furniture. It's been closed all winter. So, there's still a little nip in the air inside. But I turned up the heat and made sure the water was running okay."

"Thank you. We appreciate that." Charlie turned around and took a deep breath of the cool, pine-scented air. The cabin sat halfway up a hill. Looking out over the tops of the evergreen trees, Charlie could see the soft blue mountains stretching into the distance and the gorge where the nearby river ran. "My gosh, it's beautiful here."

"Well, we like it," Marion mused.

Charlie noticed a trail leading through the trees at the edge of the cabin's tiny yard. "Where does that trail lead?"

"Well, either up the mountain or down toward the

river. Just depends on whether you turn right or left," Marion said, using a matter-of-fact tone.

"How far up does the mountain go?" Jen asked.

"Another mile or so," Marion said. "There are a couple more cabins nestled up there."

"And we can get to the river directly from here?" Daphne asked.

"Yes. But you'll want to make sure you stay on this side of the river. It's been a warm winter, so not much snow, but we've had plenty of rain lately and the river is higher than normal," Marion added.

A distant ping went off in Charlie's head and she looked at the woman squarely. There was something Marion was specifically not saying. An image of thick trees with a tangled canopy flashed through Charlie's mind and a sharp, cold pang filled her chest. "What's on the other side of the river?"

"Oh, you don't want to go over there." Marion's lips curved into an awkward smile. "The trees are thick and there's lots of dead-fall. People have gotten hurt or lost in those woods."

"Devil's Snare?" Daphne sounded more intrigued than wary.

Marion shifted her feet and glanced over toward the path. "Yes, that's what they call it."

"Is it true that if people go in they don't come out?" Daphne asked.

"People get lost all the time in the woods but most of the time they're found. A little tired, a little hungry, a little scared. I don't think we've had anybody completely disappear in those woods in probably a good ten years."

Charlie's internal lie detector went off again. She forced a smile. "Is there anything else we should be careful of?"

Marion's round, weathered face softened. "No, not really. Just that check out is at nine AM Saturday morning. I've left a little map on the dining table inside with instructions on how to get to my office, and you can drop off the key in the box attached to the door if I'm not there."

"Thank you so much for everything," Daphne said.

"Well, thank you ladies for renting from us. There's a local grocer down the mountain—DuPont's. Or you can go toward Hendersonville and find a regular supermarket."

"Okay, wonderful." Jen planted her hands on her slim hips.

"There are also couple of restaurants downtown that are pretty good. Garamond's Café is one of my favorites. And if you're looking for fancier fare, there's Springhill Restaurant and Spa. It overlooks the river and is a little more expensive, of course, but it's nice. Real nice."

"Well, thank you. We really appreciate the suggestions," Charlie said.

"Anytime. And don't hesitate to call me if you have any questions."

Daphne smiled. "We won't." The three women watched as Marion made her way down the steps, got into her truck and took off slowly down the precarious driveway.

"Okay, let's unpack the car." Jen clapped her hands together. "Then I want to go to the grocery store and get supplies."

"And margarita mix," Lisa chimed in.

"And we should fire up that hot tub too," Daphne said, pointing to the covered tub on the end of the porch overlooking the view.

"Sounds like a plan," Charlie said, heading back to the car to unload the suitcases from the back of the SUV.

THE BLENDER WHIRRED, PULVERIZING THE ICE AND RUM that Jen added to a slurry of mint, sugar syrup and lime juice. When she seemed satisfied with the results, she poured the frozen Mojito mixture into four cocktail glasses and topped each one with a fresh mint leaf.

"Charlie, can you help me carry these outside?" Jen asked.

"Of course." Charlie threw the towel in her hands over her shoulder and grabbed two of the glasses. Jen took the other two, and they headed out to the front porch.

Lisa and Daphne had already turned on the hot tub and lowered themselves into it. The six-foot diameter round tub was sunken into the porch and only a foot-tall lip protruded, reminding Charlie of an oak bucket.

Lisa was submerged up to her neck and leaned against the hot tub wall with her eyes closed. Daphne sat up straighter, holding the travel book just above the water, reading it intently.

"Daphne, put that away," Jen scolded as she leaned down and handed Daphne her drink. "We can look up things to do later."

"There are some gem mines not too far from here. You can buy a bucket of dirt and pan through it." She closed the book and rested it on top of the hot tub. Daphne took a long sip and winced, grabbing her forehead. "Brain freeze."

"Sip it slower," Lisa said not opening her eyes.

Jen carefully stepped down onto the round ledge of the tub's seating before letting herself slip up to her waist into the steaming, bubbling water. She took a seat between Lisa and Daphne, settling her back against one of the jets.

"Here ya go." Charlie handed Lisa her drink.

Lisa sat up and took the glass. She took a cautious sip then let out a deep breath. "I could get used to this."

"I don't think there's room on your balcony for a hot tub," Daphne quipped. She balanced her glass on the edge of the hot tub and picked up her book again. She slipped the second book she'd brought from the inside the cover and began to read.

"And it's too hot for one of these most of the year," Jen added.

"I know," Lisa said. "Still, it's nice."

Charlie stepped into the hot water and carefully lowered herself to the seat opposite Daphne. She sipped on her drink and let the hot water rush around her body, relaxing her tight muscles. "So, what's so interesting about that book you can't put it down?"

"I don't know. It's just really sad, I guess. This poor girl was blamed for something she didn't even do."

Lisa took another sip of her Mojito. "Well, people are ignorant and superstitious."

Daphne closed the books and put them back on the ledge. "One legend says she didn't really die, and that she lures people onto her property and feasts on them," Daphne said, sounding simultaneously titillated and horrified.

"Well, of course, she does," Lisa said sarcastically. "What witch doesn't resort to cannibalism?"

Charlie put her drink on the tub's ledge and scooted to the end of the seat, submerging her shoulders under the water. Her cheeks filled with heat despite the cool outdoor air. "Do you think there's a candy house involved?"

Jen giggled. "Yes, I'm sure there's candy involved."

"Oh, my god, you've had two sips of your drink and you're already drunk." Lisa sounded appalled, but the curve of her mouth gave her away. She continued to tease her sister. "What a lightweight."

"Well, we can't all be a lush like you," Daphne snapped.

"Hey!" Lisa sat up straight, splashing hot water on Jen and Charlie. "Just because I drink a couple glasses of wine a week doesn't make me a lush."

"Come on, you two," Charlie said. "This is supposed to be a relaxing, non-stressful week."

"You're right." Daphne shook her head, blinking. "I don't know where that came from. I don't think you're a lush. Snappish, maybe. Definitely a know-it-all," she said. "But not a lush. I'm sorry."

"Okay." It took a minute for Lisa to stop frowning and relax back into the water again.

"Say you forgive her," Jen said.

"What?" Lisa looked at Jen as if she'd grown a second head.

"Say you forgive her." Jen repeated. "She just apologized."

"Fine." Lisa rolled her eyes. "I accept your apology. You're forgiven."

"Thank you." Daphne jutted her chin in a self-satisfied way. She trained her blue-green eyes on Charlie and smiled slyly. "Speaking of forgiving, when are you going to forgive Tom?"

"Yeah, Charlie?" Jen asked. "When are you going forgive Tom?"

"I don't know. Maybe never. Why do you care?" Charlie pulled her legs up close to her chest. Her knees protruded from the water and the cool air struck her skin, causing immediate goose bumps.

"He always looks so mopey when he comes into the café." Jen's speech slurred a little.

"Well, he's a lying liar, so he may win you over with his mopey face, but he's not gonna win me." Charlie straightened her back in defiance.

"You know, nobody shows their real face," Daphne said. "Trust me. I'm queen of glamours. I personally don't blame him for keeping it from you."

"Well, I do."

"He is a nice guy," Jen mused. Her eyes blinked long and slow. "He always over-tips too."

"Come on. Y'all can't be serious," Lisa piped up. "He's a reaper and he's immortal. You can't have a relationship with an immortal. How does that end?"

"Exactly. And he lied," Charlie added.

"And he lied!" Lisa said. "That's three strikes right there."

"None of those things make him evil," Jen said.

"Everybody lies."

"I know that." Charlie sighed. "I just wish...I wish he'd been honest."

"Right, because that would've gone over well." Daphne scoffed. She adjusted her voice and cadence. "Hi, I'm Tom. I'm a reaper. Would you like to go to dinner with me? Oh, and by the way, this is what I look like when I don't have my human mask on."

Charlie made a disgusted sound in the back of her throat.

"Well?" Lisa frowned.

"You jumping on me too?" Charlie sniped.

"Nope." Lisa shook her head. "It's your life. You get to decide who you let into it." She shrugged one shoulder. "Tom may be a nice guy. But he's also dangerous. Not because he has evil in his heart, but because he's a powerful immortal creature. And he knows that, which is why he lied." Lisa sighed and blew out a breath. "Now, who's to say he wouldn't have told you eventually." Charlie opened her mouth to protest and Lisa held up one finger pointed to the ceiling. "But. He didn't. He betrayed you. And if you feel like you can't ever trust him again, then hell, no, don't forgive him. I personally like a good grudge."

Charlie's lips twisted into a scowl and she sighed. "You think I'm being stupid."

"No, I do not. He's too close to death for my comfort zone. You don't know what that would mean for you. Witches may be able to live a long time, but that doesn't mean you aren't mortal." Lisa sniffed. "And, anyway, somebody has to support you."

"Figures," Daphne said rolling her eyes. She picked up her glass and took a sip of her Mojito. "You just like being contrary."

Lisa made a face at her younger cousin. "You know what? I think we should all just forget about men and work. Concentrate on relaxing and reconnecting with this gorgeous forest and mother goddess. That's what we're here for, isn't it?"

"I like that." Jen said raising her glass. "To this gorgeous forest and mother goddess."

Lisa raised her glass as well "And rites of passage."

Daphne and Jen chimed in together, "And rites of passage." The three of them shifted their gazes to Charlie, pausing before clinking their glasses together to see if she would join in. She looked from Daphne to Lisa to Jen and her lips curved into a smile. Finally, she picked up her glass and held it up.

"To rites of passage. May they be short and painless." She leaned in and clinked her glass with theirs. They all laughed and took a sip.

Lisa swallowed back the rest of her drink. "Okay," she said. "Who wants another one?"

CHAPTER 5

Charlie awoke early the next morning, ambled down to the kitchen and made a large pot of coffee. The blender was still in the sink so she washed it up and put it back on its base. She had stopped drinking last night after her second Mojito. But her cousins had moved on to frozen margaritas and continued to drink into the night. They would probably need to sleep it off for most of the morning, which was fine with her. She liked quiet mornings to herself.

She fried an egg in a small nonstick frying pan that she found in one of the cabinets next to the stove and popped two pieces of bread into a toaster on the counter. Jen had bought already cooked bacon, and she threw a couple of pieces into the frying pan to warm them up. After she assembled her bacon and egg sandwich, she took her coffee and food out to the little table on the front porch. The chilly air pressed against her cheeks and the inside of her nose. She breathed in the cool woods and admired the green buds on the trees promising spring and life. There was no street noise. No cars or trucks. Only the sounds of birds and very faint rushing water. The river was close to the property.

After she finished up her sandwich and coffee, she dressed warmly in a pair of jeans, a T-shirt, a flannel shirt, and her waterproof barn jacket. Her camera bag sat perched next to her purse on one of the barstools and she dug through it. Her fingers grazed the box holding the tool and compass Scott had given her. She pulled it from within the bag and shoved the tool and compass into her inner pocket. The she slung her camera bag over her shoulder and scribbled off a note on a scrap pad by the ancient telephone on the breakfast bar. Lastly, she tucked her phone into her bra and headed out. The sun was not quite up in the sky yet, and she wanted to see sunrise over the river.

Charlie walked toward the path leading into the woods from the cabin's yard. A circle of large river rocks surrounded the cabin and strangely reminded Charlie of a salt circle. Before crossing over it onto the path, she stooped down.

"Magic gives off an energy signature." Evangeline's voice rang through her head. Her aunt had held up a hand-carved wand made of ash wood. She had placed the wand in Charlie's palm during one of their training sessions. "Once you fully accept your power as a witch you'll become more attuned to it," Evangeline had said. "You'll be able to recognize from sight or touch whether something's been imbued with magical properties through a spell. Or whether it has it on its own."

Charlie shook off the memory and hovered her palm over the flat gray river stone at her feet. She closed her eyes and waited for...what? A tingling? A chill? Nothing. She laughed out loud. It was just a circle. Probably somebody put it there because they thought it was pretty. She shook her head and stepped over the line of rocks and headed down the hill.

It took a while to wind her way down the path toward the river. It had rained recently and there were muddy slippery stretches. Twice she almost lost her balance. Finally, the trees opened up to an embankment. Dark water flowed in the expanse of the river. In some places, the current swirled. Charlie went left and followed the riverbank toward the sound of a waterfall. She took her camera from its bag and cautiously made her way down the bank. Several slabs of granite lined the top of the falls causing a drop-off, and the water emptied into the fast-moving current below. When she got to the bottom of the falls, she took photos. Making adjustments to blur the water then to capture it in a freeze-frame action. The sky lightened to a dull gray. She'd make sure to check the weather later. Maybe they weren't going to get any sun today.

A deer wandered out onto the opposite bank and Charlie raised her camera to her eye again, zooming in on the beautiful creature and the two fawns following it. She fired off several shots.

Something white flashed across the lens, startling her. Her finger automatically held down the shutter, firing off three more shots before Charlie lowered the camera to find the source of the motion. The deer disappeared back into the safety of the trees. She scanned the bank looking for whatever had spooked the deer, half-hoping to see a bear. Instead, she found a girl standing near the top of the falls wearing a dirty white nightgown. Pine straw and sticks jutted from her long, dark, tangled hair. The translucence of the girl's skin gave her away even before an icy finger of dread touched Charlie's heart.

The girl couldn't have been more than fourteen or fifteen, and she would never get any older. Charlie's heart thudded in the back of her throat as she raised one hand in a wave to the girl. The child's black eyes stared at her for a moment, but her face showed no acknowledgment of Charlie's gesture. Instead, she turned and headed back into the woods. Charlie pulled her phone from her front pocket. Only one bar flickered in and out so making a phone call would be iffy, but she might be able to get a text through. She thumbed Jason's contact info and pressed send text.

Can you do a missing person's search for me?

She waited a moment, watching the screen. Finally, an ellipsis appeared indicating he was responding.

Aren't you on vacation?

Not from dead people.

You want me to find a dead person who is missing?

Yes. A girl. Maybe 14 or 15. Dark hair. Wearing a nightgown. Maybe she was kidnapped or something?

And this would be where exactly?

The mountains in North Carolina. Near Eddington.

I love how you think I'm some sort of miracle worker and can just dig up missing people for you. Especially without a name.

Oh, for pity's sake, I know you have a database you can search. Several, actually. Stop giving me a hard time.

LOL. I have actual cases, you know. Inside my own state.

Yes. I know. I also know you like helping me.

An eye-rolling emoji appeared, and Charlie laughed out loud. She could almost hear him blowing hot air through his flared nostrils as he uttered the words that appeared on the screen.

Fine. I'll see what I can find.

Thank you! You're the best.

A cold chill settled around Charlie's shoulders, and she could feel the girl's eyes on her. She looked through the telephoto lens again, zooming it to the largest setting of 300 mm. She used it to scan the bank of the other side of the river. There were no dark shadows. No flashes. Why was the girl on the other side of the river? Why had she retreated into the forest? When most spirits realized Charlie could see them, they would do whatever they could to move closer, to have a conversation. Most spirits, she found, were lonely.

Charlie's breath caught in her throat for a moment as a dark form came into focus beneath the canopy of trees. Maybe if they went into town today, she would stop by Marion's office and ask more questions. She drew the camera away from her face and squinted, trying to see the girl with her naked eye. But she only saw murky darkness there.

Charlie's phone vibrated in her pocket and she pulled it out. She had a new text from Jen.

Where are you?

Down by the river.

Why didn't you wake me?

I figured after last night you'd want to sleep in. LOL.

No. I'm fine. I took an aspirin and drank a ton of water before going to sleep.

What about Lisa and Daphne?

They're still sleeping. They will definitely be hungover. They laughed at me last night.

LOL. Then it serves them right.

Come back. We could go into town and grab an early lunch or a late breakfast.

Cool. I want to stop by Marion's office and maybe the library.

Okay. Is Google broken?

I need information that's not found online. Newspaper archives for the local area.

Why do you suddenly need to look something up?

Spirit encounter. Want to see if I can find anything about her.

Friendly?

Not sure. Only saw her for a minute. She looks young though.

Okay. Come back and we'll go.

Should be there in about thirty minutes, the path is slick and muddy.

See you soon. Be careful of the path and the spirit!

Will do.

Charlie tucked her phone into her pocket and put her camera into its case and started to climb back up the incline by the waterfall. The way the water from the cascade struck the still flowing river caused a mist to rise. The soft spray of water made the exposed earth muddier and the moss-covered granite slick. Charlie's foot slipped, and she landed on all fours. Her fingernails dug into the mud and her palms stung from the impact against rough pebbles. Wet mud penetrated her jeans at the knees and coated her hands and the spray from the river coated her backside.

"Dammit."

She would have to take a shower and put on clean clothes once she got back. Something cold touched the back of her neck sending a quiver shimmying through her. Her heartbeat sped up, and she looked up. The girl from the other side of the river stood directly in front of her. Charlie's heart slammed into her throat and she lurched backward, almost losing her balance. The spirit's dark gaze locked onto hers. The girl's eyes were as muddy as the earth coating Charlie's fingers but something in them blazed with a dark light. She had been startled by spirits before, unnerved and even frightened on occasion, but something about the way this girl looked at her was different from all the other spirits she had encountered. A palpable malevolence emanated from the girl.

"You see me," the girl said in an unnatural high-pitched voice. It reminded Charlie of the voices of the munchkins from The Wizard of Oz. The girl hissed, "Conduit."

Charlie tried to stand but her foot slipped again, bringing her to her knees. Her mind raced through all the possible responses. Upsetting a spirit was a dangerous prospect.

"You shouldn't be here," the girl said. "She knows about you now. She doesn't like strangers in her woods."

Those words in the girl's munchkin-like voice should have sounded comical, but instead, they hung in the air like a dark cloud, heavy and ominous.

Charlie kept her tone soft. "Let me leave and I won't come back. I promise." Cold dread snaked its way into Charlie's chest. It wrapped around her heart and squeezed tight.

The girl shifted her gaze to the forest across the river. Her stare was dreamy as if she were remembering some other time, some other life. "I'm sorry." The girl's whisper slid across Charlie's skin and her body went numb. "It's too late now."

Charlie dug her fingers into the muddy bank. The muscles in her legs twitched with adrenaline as she made a quick scan of the space between her and the path. A little voice inside her head screamed *run!* Charlie slowed her breathing, moving her body deliberately, inching up the bank. Everything hinged on getting her feet out of the mud and up this slick slope. There were only a few feet between her and a granite slab jutting up a few inches. Even with the moss covering it, she would have better traction than the mud. The girl drifted right as if she'd read Charlie's thoughts. Charlie swallowed hard and forced herself to meet the girl's black eyes. The girl's expression shifted from dreamy to deadly in the space of a second. "She wants you. Nothin' I can do about that now, Conduit."

Charlie took a sidestep, getting one foot onto a small mound of grass jutting from the bank. "I can help you, you know. Help you find the light and leave her far behind."

The girl's face shifted again, and she trained her black fire eyes on Charlie. "There is no light. Only the dark. Only these woods."

A fresh shiver shook Charlie to the core. A long pause filled up the space between them. Charlie opened her mouth to continue bargaining. Maybe she could convince the spirit to let her go. The words died in her throat when she heard a low growl coming from the girl. The girl raised her arms in front of her and made a pushing motion forward. A sharp pain hit Charlie in the middle of her chest just before she found herself flying backward. A thousand needles pricked her skin when she landed in the frigid water. She struggled against the fast-moving current and the weight of her wet clothes. She struggled to tread water, but the current yanked her under, swirling her body. The cold sank into her flesh making it even harder to move. The air in her lungs grew stale. Her lungs ached. She kicked as hard as she could and finally broke the surface again gulping in air and spitting water.

The bank looked different. How far had she traveled? Up ahead a drop-off loomed. It was not as steep as the one she'd been pushed into, but the water rushing over it moved even faster, crashing into large rocks downstream.

Charlie kicked harder but with each stroke of progress the current pulled her toward the next waterfall. She turned on her back, staring at the sky. God, this was not how things were going to end for her. Not today.

She righted herself and kicked, swimming closer to the bank. Her foot scraped the bottom of the pebble-covered incline, and for a second, she tasted freedom. She didn't know how she would get past the spirit, but if she could at least make it to the path, she would find a way.

Something icy brushed against her leg and Charlie struggled harder to reach the shore. The sensation of fingers wrapping around her ankle sent sharp pinpricks of pain up her leg. She kicked at it, trying to free herself but one hard yank pulled Charlie beneath the surface, down below the rushing current into the darkness.

JEN PACED BACK AND FORTH ON THE FRONT PORCH OF THE cabin, stopping every few moments to stare at the opening of the trail head leading into the forest.

The front door behind her opened and closed. Her sister Lisa walked across the porch and leaned against the log banister with her arms folded across her chest. "I don't think any amount of staring at that path is going to actually make her show up."

"She said she'd be half an hour." Jen pulled her

phone from her back pocket and glanced at the time. She whipped off another text to Charlie and waited, watching the small screen in her hand.

"I'm sure she's fine. She said it was muddy, right? I mean, if it's an incline and it's muddy it could just be taking her longer."

"It's been two hours. She should just text me back, dammit. This isn't like her."

Lisa sighed and rubbed the top of her sister's arm. A gesture of comfort that Lisa rarely displayed. "We could go looking for her. If you want."

The knot in Jen's stomach tightened. Why did that make her feel worse? "What if we don't find her?"

"Don't be an idiot. We will. We'll probably run into her on the path, covered in mud from having to climb up a steep hill."

"Really? You think so?"

"I do. Then you can give her hell for not texting you back. Okay?"

"Okay." Jen forced a smile. That knot in her stomach still didn't let go.

"Cool. Let's do this." Lisa jerked her thumb toward the front door. "I'll go grab Daphne and my coat."

"Sounds good." Jen waited until the door shut behind her sister before whipping off another text.

Hi. Got a sec?

She rocked on her feet and concentrated on the tiny screen. Her heart thudding lightly in her throat. Finally...

Sure. How are the mountains?

Not sure. Charlie went for a walk. Said she'd be back in half an hour. But it's been two.

Charlie's very levelheaded. I'm sure she's fine.

I know. I just have a sick feeling in my stomach. Something's not right.

What can I do?

Do you know anybody in this area? You know, just in case. Just in case, what?

Maybe Lisa was right. Maybe she was worrying about nothing.

I don't know. I'm probably just being silly.

Okay. Here's what I'll do. I'll check around and see what I can come up with.

That'd be great.

Keep me updated.

I will. Thank you!

She signed off with the smiley emoji just as Lisa walked out onto the porch.

"Is that Charlie?" Lisa craned her neck to get a glimpse of her sister's phone.

"No. I was just checking the weather," Jen lied.

Lisa narrowed her eyes. "Okay..."

"What? I wanted to see if it's gonna rain."

"All right. Calm down. Nobody's accusing you of anything."

"I know..." Jen sighed and tucked her phone in her bra. "I'm just edgy, that's all."

Lisa rolled her eyes and handed her sister a small velvet pouch. "Maybe this'll help."

Jen wrapped her fingers around the pouch and the contents shifted. "You expect us to need these? They're for Charlie's ceremony."

Lisa shrugged. "No. But I know they make you feel better."

Jen loosened the drawstring and touched the stones inside. A cool calm spread through her, and she closed her eyes for a moment, breathing in and out, taking in the healing energy. After a minute, she tightened the string and slipped the bag into the pocket of her coat.

"Better?" Lisa asked.

"Better." Jen smiled and glanced at the door. "Where's Daphne?"

"She's not coming. She said somebody needed to stay here in case we disappeared too."

"Well, that's cheerful," Jen muttered under her breath and followed Lisa down the steps.

"Honestly, I think she's so hungover she can't stand the thought of putting on real clothes."

"Why are you not more hungover? You drank more than all of us."

Lisa laughed. "I drink more than you guys do."

"Oh." Jen frowned. "Are you trying to tell me something? Should I be worried?"

"Of course not. I'm the only female partner in a law firm full of men who like to drink scotch. Once you build up a tolerance, fruity drinks really don't touch it. Especially when they're made by your lightweight sister," Lisa teased as they made their way onto the path.

Jen gave Lisa a side-eyed glance and saw her mouth curve up into a smirk. She rolled her eyes and brought her attention back to the path. "It's muddier than I thought it was going to be."

"Why? Charlie already told you it was muddy."

"I don't know," Jen said. "It didn't look that bad from the cabin." Jen glanced up at the sky. Gray clouds moved overhead giving the forest an eerie preternatural glow. Jen couldn't see spirits the way Charlie did, but her witch's senses were heightened, and the hair on the back of her neck and arms stood up, sentinels warning her to pay attention. Shadows played at the corners of her eyes but they disappeared as soon as she glanced their way. Was this how Charlie saw the world, shadows dancing just out of view?

Lisa seemed less concerned, which comforted Jen. She could always count on her sister to keep a level head in any situation. They walked in silence following the long trail toward the river. Overhead, a crow cawed and

Jen shifted her gaze toward the bird. It batted its black glossy wings and flew ahead of them. It glided back and forth, staying in their line of sight. Jen opened her mouth to comment on it, but Lisa cut her off.

"It's been following us since we left the front porch." Lisa's foreboding tone made the hair on Jen's arms stand up.

"What?" Jen's heart sped up and the crisp air chilled the inside of her nose as she breathed it in too fast. "Why?"

"I don't know yet."

Jen trained her eye on the bird, despite her sister's warning. "What should we do?"

"I don't want to spook you any more than you already are, but she's indebted to someone and shrouded."

"How do you know that?"

Lisa gave her a how-do-you-think scowl.

"Can you tell if it's..." The words died on her lips but she finished the thought in her head. *Evil?*

Lisa shook her head. "I wish I'd brought my wand."

A chill skittered through Jen and she shivered at her sister's words. Evangeline had taught them all when they were girls that wands were not used in everyday magic, no matter what the storybooks said. They magnified a witch's abilities and allowed the focus of energy. "That kind of power can be too much for most witches," Evangeline had told them. "You should only use a wand for high holidays and certain rites. They're not for playing. You girls understand me? You are never to point your wand at someone and cast with it."

Jen shoved her hands deeper into her coat pocket and tightened her grip on the pouch. Her fingers tingled a little, and she scoured the ground looking for something specific. When she spotted the fallen branch from what looked like a hickory tree, she left the path. Carefully, she surveyed the twigs jutting from it for just the right size before she pressed her foot against the larger central branch and snapped off a limb. She plucked the few dead brown leaves still clinging to it and broke off any smaller offshoots until it was clean. Then she snapped the wood in half, leaving her with two thin lengths of wood, each roughly ten inches long.

Lisa had stopped and watched her sister with a curious expression.

"Here you go." Jen handed one of the straight green twigs to her sister. "Not perfect, but it will do in a pinch."

Lisa wrapped her hand around the base of the makeshift wand and snapped it back and forth. It made a swishing sound. "What do you have in that pouch?"

Jen pulled her velvet bag from her pocket and untied the gold drawstring, carefully opening it. The cache of various stones and crystals sparkled a little even in the dim light. She plucked a flat black stone about the size of her thumbnail and handed it to Lisa.

Lisa placed the stone flat in the palm of her hand, pressed the end of the stick against the stone, and wrapped her hand around it. She again cut through the air with the wand and a translucent pale blue smoke appeared from the tip. Lisa shifted her gaze to her sister's face, concern etching lines into her forehead. "What about you?"

Jen picked through the stones until she found a piece of dark green jade. She pulled the drawstring tight and slipped the bag back into her pocket. She placed the stone in her palm and held the wand against it tightly in a clenched fist. She whipped the twig back and forth and uttered an incantation. A glowing green smoke trail followed the swirl she cut through the air. "I'm good."

A loud cawing made them both look up just in time to see the large bird headed straight for their heads. Jen's heart leapt into her throat and she held her wand up, but Lisa had already swiped at the air forming a series of zigzags. The bird struck the protective net of magic. Tangled, the bird lost its momentum and plummeted to the ground with a flat thud. Lisa walked over to it, her face determined and fearless. She pointed her new wand at the bird.

"Who do you belong to?" she asked.

The bird struggled against an invisible force holding its wings close to its body. It tried to hop away, but Lisa swiped at it again, binding its feet, forcing it onto its side.

82

It cawed one last time and then grew very still. One black jewel of an eye trained on Lisa, unblinking.

"Is it dead?" The thought of killing something, even out of self-defense put a sour taste in her mouth and she grimaced.

"No, it's not dead." Lisa wore an expression of heavy concentration. The bird struggled to break free of the invisible force holding her down, but Lisa made a circle with the tip of her wand and the bird flattened against the ground. "She's under a spell. Won't talk."

"Poor little thing." Jen knelt next to it but didn't get too close. "It's not her fault. Maybe if we freed her from the spell, she'd feel indebted to us."

"It would take three of us to break the spell. We need Daphne."

"Okay." Jen shifted her gaze to her sister's face. "What do you wanna do?"

"Well," Lisa sighed, "if we let it go, it's just gonna run to its master."

"Or mistress." Jen looked toward the path in front of them. The heavy cold feeling of dread flooded into her belly. "A witch."

"Yep. A dark witch," Lisa said, sounding annoyed.

"Do you think it ties back into that book of Daphne's?"

"Maybe. I mean, there's truth in every legend," Lisa

repeated Daphne's words from the day before, her face solemn.

"What if we let it go but did a silencing spell? That could at least buy us some time. And I can do that with just the stones I have."

"What else do you have in that bag of yours?" Lisa asked, nodding at Jen's pocket.

Jen pulled the velvet bag from her pocket again. Quickly untying the drawstring and flattening the bag into her palm, she placed the two jade stones back among the others. "That's all I've got. I wasn't expecting to have to cast for anything."

Lisa picked over the stones. "We have enough to make a binding circle."

"I don't like this. I don't like this at all." Jen shook her head.

"Well, it's too dangerous to just free it. Not until we know exactly what we're dealing with." Lisa's gaze locked on Jen's.

Jen took a deep breath and began pulling stones that would bind the bird to the ground. She knelt and placed seven of her stones in a circle around the bird, being careful not to get too close to its sharp beak. It attempted to fluff its wings, but Lisa's spell held it tight. It made a gurgling sound deep in its throat that reminded Jen of a growl. One black eye stared at Lisa. Crows had excellent memories and unless they could turn this one, it would always remember Lisa's actions against it. If they freed it now, not only would it run to its mistress and announce their arrival, it would more than likely return and continue to target Lisa. Images of Alfred Hitchcock's movie *The Birds* flashed through Jen's mind and she shivered. What if it brought friends?

"You know this is why I don't like birds, right?" Jen said.

"Tell that to your flock of chickens."

"Chickens are different," Jen said. "They have personalities."

"Huh," Lisa said with a trace of irony in her voice. "I'll remember that."

When she laid the last stone into place, Jen hopped up and took a step back. She had retained her jade stone. She pressed the cold gem against her palm and wrapped her hand around the wand again.

"Okay, let's do this," Lisa said, sounding as if she were trying to psyche herself up a little. She took the tip of her wand and circled it over the top of the stones, drawing it into a spiral. Jen could see the wispy blue smoke of energy swirling like an inverted vortex. Her sister's lips moved, but Jen could barely hear her as she uttered the spell to hold the bird captive. When she was done Lisa dropped her hand and stepped back next to her sister. The bird hopped up immediately, staring at Lisa with blazing black eyes. It opened its black beak and cawed in protest.

"Oh, stop your squawking," Lisa said, "before I bind that beak of yours closed."

"Lisa," Jen scolded. "She doesn't mean that, Ms. Crow."

"Oh, for cryin' out loud, it's just a bird." Lisa protested.

"She didn't mean that, Ms. Crow," Jen said again.

"Come on," Lisa complained. "We need to go find out what happened to Charlie. We've wasted enough time on this."

Jen nodded and gave the bird one last sad look. How young had it been when the witch who possessed it put it under her spell? She hated to see anything suffer and there was nothing worse for a wild thing than to be taken captive. Jen stepped up her pace to catch up with her sister. "Promise me we'll try to free it."

"We'll do what we can for it. But it may not want to be freed."

"Okay. That's all I ask," Jen said.

"It's just..." Lisa cast a quick glance over her shoulder, "...a dark thing like that."

"I know." Jen nodded. Panic tickled the back of her throat. "Charlie."

JEN WALKED ALONG THE BANK OF THE RUSHING RIVER scanning the ground for any sign of Charlie. Panic pressed on her shoulders and chest. Boot prints cut into the mud, and foot-shaped shadows where the soil was not so wet led them toward the waterfall. She paused to look over the steep embankment. Had Charlie moved down near the water? Why would she?

"There's nothing up that way," Lisa said, coming up from behind her. "Have you found anything?"

"Footprints. But I can't be certain they're hers."

"Let's keep moving." Lisa held out her hand and pulled her sister back away from the edge the bank.

Something cold touched the back of Jen's neck, sending a shiver crawling down her spine. It was the distinct feeling of being watched. She stopped in her tracks and glanced around.

"What's wrong?" Lisa asked.

"I don't know." Jen's eyes narrowed as she surveyed the woods across the river, looking for the source.

"What?" Wary panic filled Lisa's tone and her whole body stiffened. She shifted her gaze to the woods. "Do you see anything?"

Jen shook her head. "No. Charlie mentioned she'd run into a spirit, so maybe that's what it is."

"Or maybe not." Lisa pursed her lips. Her knuckles whitened, and she pulled her makeshift wand in close to her body. She shifted her gaze back to her sister. "Let's keep going."

Jen tightened her grip on her wand as well and readied herself. *For what? What are you going to do battle with? An unseen specter?*

The chill continued to cling to her body, but they moved on. Every nerve sang with awareness.

The sound of the water grew louder as they approached the waterfall. Jen's breath caught in her throat when she saw the scarred embankment. There were clear hand prints and deep depressions in the mud. Jen knelt as close to the edge of the embankment as she dared. She uttered the words before she could really process them. "She fell into the river."

"No. No way." Lisa pointed at the dark red clay midway down the bank. "From the way those hand prints are facing she's climbing back up. It doesn't look like she slid down any farther than right there."

"She fell in. I can feel it."

"Take a breath, Jen. You're letting your imagination run away with you."

"We need to tell someone. Get some help." Jen rose to her feet. The panic in her chest fluttered against her ribcage and she thought she might be sick.

"There's no evidence she fell." Lisa touched Jen's elbow and used her calming voice. The one Jen heard her use when talking to people about their taxes.

"I know, but..."

A loud caw announced a crow just as he swooped down from the other side of the river. It dived at them and Jen quickly knelt and covered her head with one hand. When the bird turned and started to make another pass Lisa raised her wand and carved an X in the air. The thin trails of blue light lingered just long enough for the X to imprint itself on the backs of Jen's eyelids. She blinked it away just in time to watch a strong wind lift up the river. It flowed violently through the trees, causing leaves to swirl, forcing the crow off course. Another swipe from Lisa's wand and the large wave crested just high enough to wash over the bird's feet. It took a moment for it to flap its way above the water. Its black feathers grazed against the top of the wave, and it flew up and over the waterfall. Their gaze followed it until it disappeared into the trees on the other side of the river. The wave carried over the falls with a crash and the river flowed as if nothing had happened.

"That bird belongs to the same entity the other does," Lisa said. "It's following orders."

Jen folded her arms across her chest and hugged herself tightly. "How do you know that?"

"It's not shrouded. It showed me what happened. Charlie didn't fall," Lisa said.

Jen's stomach turned into an icy rock. She dropped to her knees and locked gazes with her sister.

"She was pushed. Somebody wanted her in that water."

"Who?" Jen asked, getting to her feet again.

"I don't know." Lisa said. "Whoever it is, it's not..."

"What? Stop doing that." Jen scolded. "You're freaking me out."

Lisa frowned and met her sister's gaze. "It's not human. At least not in the sense of normal human."

"You think it's the spirit she met?"

"I don't know. I've never heard of a spirit powerful enough to control crows. Makes me wonder what else it can control."

"Well, if that book is right, maybe it's the spirit of a witch." Jen stepped away from the embankment wanting to put some space between her and the river.

Lisa followed close behind. "Maybe...or maybe it's a demon."

"Well, either way, we're gonna need help."

Lisa nodded in agreement. "Let's go mobilize Daphne and call Evangeline."

"Okay. What about the sheriff? Do we involve him or just handle this on our own?"

Lisa cast a glance over her shoulder, still watchful and wary. "What are the pros?"

Jen shrugged "The police will know the area?"

"True," Lisa said. "And the cons?"

"There's a lot we can't control by involving other

people. And until we know who or what we're dealing with..."

"I agree." Lisa nodded. "But they may have resources we don't." She wrapped her arms around her slim waist, hugging them tightly to her body.

"Maybe what we need is somebody who speaks their language. Somebody who can run interference for us if we need it." Jen's lips curved up, and she met Lisa's gaze. "Jason."

Lisa nodded. "Jason."

CHAPTER 6

B y the time Jason got to the café, Evangeline was already heading out the door. He called to her on the street just before she turned down the alleyway leading to the back of the building. When she looked at him, her blue eyes burned wild and bright. It was a look that could stop a Mack truck on a dime. Her usually neat silver hair had escaped the bun she wore and jutted out in places, and the lines around her mouth deepened with sour impatience.

Despite her appearance, he cleared his throat and forced himself to keep walking. "Miss Evangeline, wait."

"Jason, I'm sorry, honey, but I don't have time right now. Miss Dottie will help you with your dinner."

"Jen called me," he blurted, then glanced around the street to see if anyone had heard him. Luckily, the few people milling around town were not paying attention to him and kept moving on to their destinations. He lowered his voice as he drew closer to her. "I know what's going on. I'm coming with you."

"Well, come on, then." Evangeline's shoulders relaxed a little, and she nodded and held up her hand and waved him on. She was so tiny and wispy Jason often thought she might blow away in a strong wind. But her sharp blue eyes told him she was not to be messed with. He was still wrapping his head around the whole witch thing, but had concluded that the Payne women might be nice as pie and use endearments like *honey* and *sweetie,* but when it came down to it, they were fierce creatures and God help anyone who got in their way. Better to be on their side than against them.

Jason stepped up his pace to keep up with her as she walked back to her old black and tan Ford F150. Her keys jangled as she pushed it into the lock on the passenger side and popped open the door for Jason.

She looked him up and down, her gaze landing on the messenger bag hanging from his shoulder. A shadow of skepticism crossed her face. "I don't know how long this is gonna take. May be a few days. Did you bring clothes?"

Jason nodded and patted the canvas bag. "Yes, ma'am."

"All right, then." She finally gave him a weary smile.

"Get in. I need to run by my condo and grab some clothes."

"Yes, ma'am."

JASON WANDERED AROUND EVANGELINE'S COZY LIVING, room admiring the photos that covered almost every inch of the long white wall that dominated the room. The photos came in many varieties, black and white, color, tintype, candid and formal. Landscapes and people. Lots of people. Most he assumed were her family. There were no knickknacks to gather dust. The only thing that came close was a willow broom hung horizontally above the sea of photos, as if it were flying above them. He understood on an intellectual level that she was a practicing witch and couldn't deny the things he'd seen, even though he really wanted to. But the idea of this tiny old woman perched on that broom, a silhouette against a full moon, her silver hair loose and whipping behind her as she zoomed about made him chuckle then shift uncomfortably. He would ask Charlie when they found her. She would be honest if he asked point blank. Do witches fly on brooms?

He moved on from the photos, stopping in front of a bookcase with glass doors that had brass locks. It reminded him of bookcases he'd seen in his cousin

Kenny's law office. Two of the doors were unlocked, waiting to be pushed closed. Evangeline had disappeared down the hallway. He could hear her rifling through drawers, talking to herself about what she needed. He bent over and peered through the glass at the old leather-bound books that took up half the shelf. All had Roman numerals on the spine and some writing in a language he didn't recognize. Was it Latin? He couldn't be sure. The other half of the shelf held a stack of small wooden boxes of various sizes, each with their own little brass padlocks, which he thought could easily be broken off.

The doorbell rang, startling him with an unpleasant jolt, and he shot up straight. He shook off the feeling he'd been caught doing something he shouldn't. After all, he was just looking at books on a shelf. Nothing to be ashamed of, really.

Evangeline called to him from down the hall., "Jason, can you please answer that?"

He cleared his throat. "Yes, ma'am." He walked over to the front door and opened it without looking through the peephole. He scowled at the sight of Tom Sharon standing with his hand held up as if to knock on the door.

"Tom," Jason said, ignoring the hair rising on the back of his neck. He knew exactly what Tom Sharon was, the same way he knew what Evangeline was. It should have scared the bejesus out of him, but it didn't. Maybe it was from his years of being a cop and knowing that every time he went to work there was a chance he could die and he'd accepted that fact a long time ago.

"What are you doing here?"

Tom glanced at the number on the front door of the condo, looked back to Jason and cocked his head, ignoring Jason's question. "This is Miss Evangeline's condo, correct?"

"Maybe," Jason said. "What are you doing here?"

"I need to talk to Miss Evangeline."

"Well, Miss Evangeline's a little busy at the moment. You'll have to come back some other time." Jason started to close the door, but Tom stuck his foot into the crack, stopping him. Jason opened the door a little and met Tom's gaze. The fire in Tom's brown eyes did not faze Jason the way Tom had evidently expected.

"It's an emergency. Please."

"You do know I have a weapon strapped to my hip, don't you?"

Tom narrowed his eyes. "And you know it can't kill me," Tom said with a smirk.

"Maybe not, but it sure as hell will hurt. A lot," Jason countered.

"Touché," Tom said. "I concede. You win the largest penis award. Now, may I please come in? This is important."

"Tom?" Evangeline said, coming up next to Jason. A flush of red colored her prominent cheekbones and she was a little breathless from rushing about. "What are you doing here?"

"Hello, Miss Evangeline. I've come to help." Tom offered up a charming smile.

Jason rolled his eyes. "Oh, Lord."

Evangeline gave Jason a sideways glance and crossed her arms. She didn't offer up her usual friendly smile. Instead, impatience crept into her voice. "I don't mean to be rude, Tom, but I really can't talk now."

"I know about Charlie," Tom said.

Evangeline's expression changed from weary patience to puzzlement. "How?"

"Jen—" Tom tipped his chin and gave her a sheepish look. "— texted me. Told me what's going on."

"Jen texted *you*?" Jason asked, not bothering to mask the irritation in his voice.

"Oh." Evangeline's hand floated to the base of her throat. "I had no idea that you and Jen were—"

"Friends. Just friends. She's been very kind to me the last few months. Please. I really do want to help."

Evangeline's slim shoulders rose and fell with a heavy sigh. "How are you gonna help us?"

"I'll talk to the reaper in the area. He'll know if Charlie is in his book and that will give us what we need to proceed."

Evangeline blanched. "His book?"

"Yes, ma'am," Tom said. "Every reaper has a book for his or her territory."

"And she's not in yours—" Evangeline couldn't seem to finish the sentence.

"No," Tom reassured her. Jason watched Tom's face for any sign he might be lying. If he was, then he was a master at it, because Jason saw no tells.

Evangeline nodded and glanced at Jason. "Well, I suppose we could always use an extra body. What do you think, Jason?"

Jason forced a smile. Dammit, he didn't want Tom on this trip. "It's your call, Miss Evangeline."

She nodded. "Okay." She looked at Tom as if making up her mind. "Well, all right then. We're leaving in a few minutes. Are you prepared for that?"

"Yes, ma'am."

Jason stepped between Tom and Evangeline and met the man's gaze. "I'm only gonna say this once. I don't know what your motive is, but if you get in our way, I will shoot you. I don't care if it kills you or not."

Evangeline gasped. Fear touched her sharp blue eyes. "Jason Tate. What would your mama say? Apologize to Tom."

Jason opened his mouth to protest but Evangeline's tone sharpened. "Right this minute. I won't have this petty macho bullshit. Do you hear me? Charlie's like one of my kids, and if you can't straighten up and be helpful, then you can just stay here." Tom snorted softly. She turned her attention to him, pointing. "That goes for you, too. Reaper or not."

Tom's face shifted from amused to contrite and he nodded. "Of course. I apologize."

Jason made a low growl in the back of his throat. He scowled. "Fine. I apologize."

"Good. Now, let's get going. We're burning daylight."

CHAPTER 7

Jen paced back and forth in front of the bench inside the small Brynn Falls police station. Daphne and Lisa sat watching her. The police station had several desks spread out behind the receptionist's desk. Two larger offices with floor-to-ceiling glass windows overlooked the whole office. The louvered shades were drawn obscuring their occupants. The stark black *Chief of Police* sign stood out against the closed white blinds on one glass-front door. The chief was hiding in there. Jen could feel it. The receptionist had put them off twice saying someone would be with them soon.

A phone rang and a uniformed officer sitting at the desk closest to the receptionist answered it.

"Maybe we should've called instead," Daphne muttered and laid her head on Lisa's shoulder. Daphne's usually perfectly styled bob was pulled away from her face with a thick leather headband and large black-framed sunglasses hid her blood-shot eyes and blocked any light that was too offensive.

Jen stopped pacing and crossed her arms. She glanced across the room. Three of the five desks were empty. Her eyes went to the closed door and the shuttered window.

"Daphne's right. This is taking too long."

"Come on. Just sit down." Lisa patted the empty place on the bench next to her. "Jason asked us to report her missing, and that's what we're gonna do."

"We're losing daylight. We could be out looking for her," Jen said, taking a seat. "Maybe Jason'll have better luck. I mean, these are his people."

"I'm not sure what that means, but okay." Lisa sounded irritated. She glanced away from Jen and whispered something into Daphne's ear. Daphne made a whiny, nasally sound but straightened up and got to her feet. She pushed her sunglasses onto the top of her head and went straight for the receptionist's desk.

"What's she doing?" Jen asked. She leaned forward straining to hear her cousin's quiet voice.

"Nothing." Lisa's gaze followed Daphne.

"Liar," Jen whispered. Daphne had her back to them. Jen watched carefully, keeping her eyes on the receptionist. The older woman's eyes glazed over as

Daphne spoke to her. Jen recognized that wide-eyed, unfocused look, but the woman rose to her feet and was halfway across the office before Jen could say stop.

Daphne returned to the bench wearing a self-satisfied smile. She sat back down on the bench next to Lisa and pushed her sunglasses back down over her eyes. "She's nice and suggestible. We should be getting some attention in three, two, one..."

A tall, brawny officer emerged from behind the door. He wore a tan uniform shirt and brown pants but looked more like he belonged on a lumberjack crew. Gray salted his dark, wavy hair. Following close behind him was a short but lean officer with a thin face made up of sharp angles. His dark, hungry eyes zeroed in on Jen, making her instinctively fold her arms across her breasts.

Lisa and Jen stood, but Daphne remained seated.

"Hello." The tall officer smiled and held out his hand as an offering. "I'm Chief Brighton," he said. "Marla said you have a missing person to report."

Lisa stepped forward and shook the chief's hand first. "Yes. Our cousin went for a walk down by the river this morning and never came back."

The chief smiled, his eyes wrinkled at the corners cutting deep lines into his cheeks. His dark blues eyes glittered like hard little sapphires but they offered no comfort. Jen shifted her feet. He gestured to the officer standing beside him. "I see. Well, this is my sergeant. Jeremy Hicks. He'll be taking your statement."

Jen glanced at Daphne, who was still sitting on the bench. She'd taken off her dark glasses and worry etched lines into her usually smooth forehead. Her fine features froze for a second, reminding Jen of the porcelain figurines her mother once collected. Her pale skin had gone even paler, and she chewed on her bottom lip.

"Daphne? You okay?" she asked softly.

Daphne nodded, but didn't take her eyes off the two officers.

"How do y'all do? If you wouldn't mind following me." He gestured back toward a hallway that ran along the side of the two officers. Jen and Lisa slung their purses over their shoulders but Daphne didn't move. Instead, she continued to stare at the young man. Her eyes were a little glassy, as if holding onto unshed tears.

Lisa bent low and looked into Daphne's face, making her cousin break her gaze. "You stay here, okay? We've got this."

Daphne gave Lisa a grateful smile and nodded. Her shoulders relaxed a little, and she leaned against the back of the bench. As crazy as Daphne made Lisa sometimes, Jen knew her sister's instinct was to protect her family.

"I'm okay," Daphne said quietly. "I want to go."

"You sure?" Lisa asked.

"Yeah." Daphne offered a weak smile. "I promise."

Lisa held her hand out and Daphne took it. She helped her cousin to her feet, and it surprised Jen that Daphne continued to hold Lisa's hand even as they followed the officer. What was it about him that frightened Daphne so badly? Daphne was not exactly a mind reader or an Empath the way Charlie was, but it didn't mean she couldn't sense things about people. Jen could not wait to get her younger cousin alone and ask her what was going through her head.

"Right through here," the officer said. He turned down another hallway and led them through a door that opened into a windowless room. A table with three chairs around it dominated the space. "I'll get another chair. Just a sec," Hicks said. He smiled, but it never touched his dark brown eyes.

Once he left the room, Lisa and Jen flanked Daphne. "What's wrong?" Lisa asked.

Daphne shook her head. "Nothing." Her eyes darted over to a long mirror hanging on the wall. "I'm fine. Still just a little hungover. That's all."

Lisa gave Jen a knowing look. Daphne had seen something but couldn't say what. Not here. Not in front of whoever was standing behind that glass watching them. When she and Lisa had returned to the cabin, they'd all taken their wands from the protective boxes where they normally kept them. Jen reached into her bag and wrapped her hand around the handle of her wand. The touch of the carved nine-inch piece of oak sent an electric tingle through her hand and up her arm. With the connection made, she started to pull the wand from her purse and focus her thoughts on what she wanted to happen. The image of the glass fogging popped into her head, and she whispered the word *obscurum*. The mirror overlooking the room turned opaque as if a shot of steam had suddenly risen from below it.

Lisa closed her eyes and mumbled a spell under her breath too. The room grew very quiet as if they'd been blanketed.

Lisa opened her eyes and set her gaze on Daphne. "Okay, spill."

Daphne opened her mouth to speak just as the door opened. Sergeant Hicks appeared, dragging a fourth chair into the room. It scraped across the floor setting Jen's teeth on edge.

"All right, then, why don't you ladies have a seat?" He walked over to the mirror and drew his finger across the surface in a straight line. Water dripped in thin trails.

"Huh. Weird," he said.

Jen held her breath, waiting for the thin line to fog up again. He wiped his wet fingers on his pants and walked to the seat facing away from the mirror. Jen's heart beat hard against her rib cage. The fog on the mirror dissipated. The spell broken. How had he done that?

Jen glanced at Lisa and then toward the mirror again.

Lisa gave her a worried look and pulled out a chair. Daphne turned an even paler shade of white. Jen touched her arm trying to imbue some comfort. Daphne stared at the sergeant's badge. Jen followed her cousin's gaze, noticing the silver five-pointed star inside a circle. A pentacle. A symbol of protection. Even law enforcement knew the power of the image.

Jen took the middle seat, facing the sergeant directly and Lisa took the seat on Jen's right. Daphne settled in to the seat on the far left closest to the door. She glanced into the hallway, swallowing hard as she watched him close the door. Jen reached over and touched her hand to Daphne's forearm. It was a gentle, soft touch, just enough to still her cousin to reassure her that nothing would happen to her here.

"So, I understand y'all want to report a missing person?" the sergeant asked. He shuffled a short stack of forms and pulled a pen from his front pocket. He clicked the ballpoint until it appeared.

"Yes," Jen said sitting up straight on the edge of the seat. "We're up here from Charleston, South Carolina. Our cousin Charlie went for a walk this morning and never came back."

He nodded and scanned Jen's face. "She went for a walk?"

"Yes." Jen nodded. She reached into her purse and pulled out a picture of Charlie. It was an old picture when she was still with Scott, and Evan was only six or seven. Jen had brought it for their ceremony. As part of the ritual to induct Charlie into their coven. Jen handed the deputy the picture.

He looked it over. "And this is recent?"

Jen frowned. "Not exactly. It's a few years old, but she still looks the same. Blonde hair. Tall. Very pretty."

"Hmmm," Hicks said. "Maybe she just got distracted on her walk. Or maybe she met someone."

"No," Lisa said. She sat up straight and used her most authoritative lawyer voice. "We walked the path and found a place where she may have slipped into the river. We walked for at least a mile, hoping to find some sort of evidence of her in the water but, unfortunately, we didn't. That's why we're here. Surely, there are people who get lost in the woods around here."

"There are." The sergeant leaned back and rested his elbow on the arm of his chair. His dark brown eyes looked over Lisa in a way that irritated Jen. He was sizing her up. Trying to determine how much of a fight she was willing to give. Well, he didn't know Lisa or her reputation as a pit bull. Once she sank her teeth into something she didn't let go.

"Well." Lisa's voice was measured and steady. "We want to file a report and we would like an officer to go out and take a look. This is pretty simple. Either you'll help us or you won't. I'm pretty sure the park service will help us if you can't."

Hicks's mouth twisted into a frown. "What time did she go for this walk?"

"Early," Jen said. "Before any of us got up. So probably before 8 a.m. She did leave a note saying she was going for a walk and that she'd be back soon. Then later, she texted me and told me she was on the way back. But she never showed up. I waited for an hour, maybe an hour and a half. I thought she wasn't that far from our cabin based on what she'd said," Jen babbled and fidgeted in her chair. "It shouldn't have taken her very long to get back even though it's rained recently, and it's muddy."

"Can I see this text?" Hicks asked.

"Um, sure. I guess." Jen's voice cracked. The text had mentioned a ghost. A dead girl.

"It's okay, Jen," Lisa said. "Show him." Lisa's gaze met hers and she gave Jen a reassuring smile. "Really."

Slowly, Jen reached into her purse and pulled out her cell phone. It only took a moment for her to find the text and she handed the phone to the deputy.

"What does this mean exactly?" the deputy asked. "A spirit encounter?"

Lisa stiffened and she set her jaw as she spoke in her most authoritative tone. "Our cousin is a psychic. And sometimes she encounters spirits."

"A psychic." Hicks scoffed and his heavy brows tugged

together. "Y'all know it's illegal to file a false claim, right? I could arrest you."

"Well, considering that I'm a lawyer, I'm quite aware of the law," Lisa said. She didn't mention that she was a lawyer in South Carolina and that she mainly handled taxes, wills, real estate and sometimes the occasional contract. That was something he didn't need to know. "And there is nothing false about this report, sergeant, and it doesn't matter what that text says. The fact remains that our cousin is lost in the woods. Now, are you going to file our report or not?"

The deputy sat up straight. The muscles in his jaw tensed. He obviously didn't like the way she spoke to him. Daphne let out a little whimper.

"What is going on with you?" Lisa snapped.

"Nothing," Daphne said, her voice growing high and loud.

Jen sighed, ignoring her sister and cousin. "I think what my sister is trying to say is that we just need some help. That's all. It's gonna be dark before we know it and we're just real worried about our cousin."

The deputy shifted his gaze from Jen to Lisa and then his eyes flitted toward the mirror. "I'll be right back."

He stood up and left the room. As soon as the door clicked closed Daphne let out a ragged breath. "He's not gonna help us."

"Why do you think that?" Lisa kept her voice low.

"His aura is black. Blackest I've ever seen. So was the Chief's," Daphne whispered.

"That doesn't mean he won't help, though, does it?" Jen whispered. She met Lisa's concerned gaze.

"I don't know. A black aura doesn't necessarily mean he's evil," Lisa said. "But...it's not good either."

"He could just be under a spell." Jen wanted to be comforting, but the words sounded hollow.

"A spell?" Daphne scoffed. "Why would anybody put them both under a spell?"

"I don't know." Lisa shook her head and sighed. "I know Jason meant well, but we should just do this on our own."

Jen nodded. "I agree. We should see if there's a local coven. They may know more. Especially if it is a spell."

"Not to be a Negative Nellie, but what if they're the ones who cast the spell?" Daphne wrapped her arms around her waist and hugged tightly.

Lisa sighed and the lines between her eyebrows grew deep when she frowned. "It's a chance we're gonna have to take."

"I agree," Jen said.

"Daphne?" Lisa asked.

Daphne hesitated then finally nodded. "Me too. Anything's better than these guys."

"Good." Lisa got to her feet and gave Daphne's arm a gentle squeeze. She walked over to the mirror and knocked, breaking any of the spell that might still be working.

Daphne shivered and Jen placed a soft hand on her shoulder. Her cousin let out a tense, measured breath.

"Come on back. I know you're out there watching," Lisa said.

In less than a second, the door opened and the sergeant and chief appeared.

"Y'all aren't leaving, are you?" The sergeant offered a half-smile. Something about it made Jen's skin crawl, and she stood, putting her body between him and Daphne. The sergeant glared at her, sizing her up with a once-over glance. She fought the urge to shiver and couldn't wait to take a shower later to wash off the grimy feeling of his eyes on her.

The chief stepped forward, wearing an alligator smile. His salted dark hair gleamed in the artificial light. His hard, bright eyes were full of intelligence. "Take their report, Hicks."

"Yes, sir," Hicks said. "Why don't y'all have a seat and we'll fill this out? Then we'll send an officer with you and contact the park service to see if they might be able to help us out."

Lisa glanced briefly at Jen and nodded. Jen sat down, and Daphne sank into the chair next to her, wearing a miserable expression.

"Fine," Lisa said.

CHAPTER 8

C harlie awoke to the acrid, smoky scent of
burning wood. She should have been cold.
Hell, she should've been dead. Instead, she
was nestled into a sleeping bag in front of a blazing fire
set inside a fire ring. She unzipped the expensive down-
filled bag and assessed the situation. Her clothes had
been stripped off and were resting over a camping chair
close enough to the fire for them to dry. She touched her
ponytail. It was still damp. Her hand immediately went to
her throat. The long silver chain with the small
medallion that Jen had given her for protection was gone.

The last thing she remembered was struggling for the
surface. Her legs and arms kicking against the current
and some unseen arm that kept pulling her down. She

had focused only on the light above emanating from the sky.

Hunger gnawed at her belly. She pressed her hand against her growling stomach. What time was it? She couldn't tell from the overcast day. She sat up and glanced around the dark gloom of the interior forest. The girl. Her breath caught in her throat at the thought. The girl had pushed her into the water. Her heart sped up, and she tried to look everywhere at once. Where was the girl now? Spirit or not, she was obviously dangerous.

Charlie climbed out of the warm sleeping bag. The crisp air around her chilled her skin and goose bumps pimpled her arms and legs. Her bare feet crunched against the gravelly surface of the fire ring and dug into the soles of her feet. She couldn't wait around here. The girl might come back. Quickly, she took several steps toward her clothes and shoes. The girl had mentioned that someone was not happy to have her nearby. *A witch?* Maybe, but Charlie was not about to stick around to find out. She touched her hands to her jeans and found them barely damp. Quickly she slid them up her legs and over her hips, buttoning them into place. Her layers, a tank top, a long-sleeved T-shirt, and a flannel shirt were in various states of dampness. The tank was driest, which made sense because it was the lightest of the fabrics. She slipped it over her head followed by the pale yellow T-shirt. Her thick socks were still very wet to the touch, and

she wrung them out as best she could before slipping
them on and sticking her feet into her squishy trail shoes.
She checked the back pocket of her jeans. Miraculously,
her phone was still there, but the water had killed it. The
black glass screen stared back at her, unblinking.
Dammit. This was a new phone too.

"You're awake," a man's voice said from behind her.
Charlie turned quickly. She glanced at the ground and
snapped up a rock.

Her blood pounded in her ears as she sized him up.
He had a boyish face, wore his curly brown hair short,
but he was tall and broad-shouldered. He easily
outweighed her by 70 pounds. "You stay right there," she
said, summoning a warning voice.

He held his hands up in surrender and gave her a
weak smile. "I'm not gonna hurt you. I promise." He took
a step closer.

Charlie clenched her jaw. What she wouldn't give for
one of her uncle's shotguns right about now. "I mean it.
Stay put."

"Okay, sorry." He smiled sheepishly. "It's just, you're
the first person I've seen in a while."

Charlie frowned. "What do you mean?"

"It seems like I've been out here alone forever. I saw
you fall into the river. Fished you out."

The whole thing reminded her too much of the way
she met Tom. "Are you a reaper?"

"I...am I a what?" Confusion clouded his dark brown eyes.

"Nothing. Never mind." She let her arm fall to her side. She glanced around. "Where are we?"

"My campsite. I've been here for..." He paused and the line between his brows grew deep as he stopped to think. "For a while, I guess. I saw you fall into the river and pulled you out before you went over the falls. You'd have been dashed to bits on the rocks if you'd reached the rapids."

Charlie shivered and glanced around. The gloom of the forest went on in every direction. She scanned the trees for the girl. "I don't hear water. How far are we from the river?"

"A way in," he said. "I figured I could get you warmed up fastest with my sleeping bag and fire."

"You...you stripped me out of my clothes." It wasn't a question. She knew the answer. Of course, he did. Who else would it have been? Her cheeks flushed with the heat of embarrassment.

"You were already on the verge of hypothermia. Leaving you in your clothes would have definitely made it worse."

The adrenaline pumping through her body made her skin twitchy, and she tightened her fingers around the rock in her hands. A million questions danced on the tip of her tongue, but she couldn't settle on just one. Her

116

thoughts kept traveling back to the girl. Where was that dead girl?

"It's not that I don't appreciate you pulling me from the river, but I'd like to go back to my cabin now. My family will be worried. So, if you would just take me back to the river I'll be on my way."

"Sure, of course. There's just one thing."

"What?"

"There's no place to safely cross the river. Not for miles."

"What? Which side of the river are we on?"

"It's kind of stupid. They call it the Devil's Snare, but really, it's fine. I've camped in these woods all my life."

Charlie's heart dropped to her stomach. *There is no light. Only the dark. Only these woods.* The girl's high voice floated through her head. "We have to get out of here."

"Okay. I understand. I'll be happy to take you back, but we'll have hike to my truck, which is even farther away than the river I'm afraid." He glanced over his shoulder. "This forest is pretty dense. It could take several hours just to cross the two miles to my truck."

Charlie glanced at the sky. A thick layer of clouds obscured the sun making it impossible to determine the time. "Well, let's get going, then."

"It's gonna be dark soon and walking through these woods is hard enough when it's light. I was thinking we just stay put tonight and we'll head out at first light."

Charlie shifted her feet. Her breath sounded harsh in her ears. "Why are you so far out?"

"I was following one of the trails. But I got curious about these woods. You know what they say about them and all." His eyes tightened and darkened as he spoke. "Turns out the rumors are true."

Daphne's voice floated through Charlie's head. *There's a place called the Devil's Snare. It's supposed to be haunted. Right up your alley.*

"What rumors?" She held her breath, her heartbeat quickening.

"You know, that it's easy to get in but hard to get out."

Charlie sighed. "So, you're lost. Is that what you're trying to tell me?"

"Not lost, exactly. Just a little off course." He sounded defensive.

"Fantastic. That is just freaking fantastic. So, we're both lost." She started to pace back and forth keeping the fire between them. "Do you have a cell phone?"

His forehead wrinkled, and he shook his head. "Um. No. Sorry. I'm not really into technology."

"Great. Do you at least know how to get back to the river? My family will come looking for me. I have no doubt about that. If we can get to the river we'll at least have a chance of seeing them on the other side. Then they can call the authorities and get us both out of here."

"Right." He nodded. "That's a good plan."

"Oh-kay, well?"

"Oh, um, it's that way about quarter of a mile." He pointed to his left. All she could see were more trees and the darkened gloom.

"Wait, you carried me that whole way?"

"I..." He kicked the toe of his boot into the leaves. "You were almost hypothermic. I didn't want you to die. I knew I could warm you up here."

Charlie dropped the rock in her hand. What an idiot she'd been. "I'm sorry. I should be thanking you. I guess I overreacted."

"No, it's totally understandable. Honestly, I'm surprised you're not more freaked out." He chuckled softly.

Charlie forced a smile. "Don't get me wrong. I'm still freaked out. There are..." She glanced around, scanning the woods. Where was the girl? This was her territory. "I just really want to go home."

"Of course." He nodded but didn't move.

"So, you said it's this way?" Charlie pointed and took a step in the direction he'd pointed to a few moments before.

"Yep." He nodded again.

Charlie's stomach growled loud enough for them both to hear and she pressed her hand against her belly.

"You're hungry?"

"A little," she lied. If given the opportunity, she would have eaten a horse.

"Hang on," he said. He looked around the ground as if he were trying to find something. Then he held up one finger and smiled. "Be right back." He disappeared into the small two-man tent nearby and returned with a backpack. He fumbled to get it open and dug out an energy bar in tan plastic wrapping. "I know it's not the same as hot food, but it's about two hundred and fifty calories." He handed her the bar, and she leaned carefully over just far enough to snatch it back from him.

She read the flavor on the package: crunchy peanut butter. Her stomach growled louder when she ripped open the plastic wrapping with her teeth. The oat and protein enriched peanut butter bar tasted a little stale, but she didn't care. She crunched through it quickly, wishing for more. She looked up, and he handed her a plastic bottle of water. The label looked worn and bleached. Maybe he had bought several cases of it and by the time he'd gotten to the last bottles the labels had started to fade. Whatever the reason, she didn't really care. She twisted off the plastic top and downed a big gulp of water.

"You want another one?" He held up another energy bar.

"Maybe for the road." She took the bar and crammed it into the pocket of her damp jeans. "I lost my camera.

But I don't remember taking off my bag. Did I come with one?"

"Right, your bag." He walked over to the camping chair, which looked a little worse for wear. Hanging off the back of it was her bag. He grabbed the strap and handed it to her. "Everything's there. I mean I did look at your wallet to see who you were, but that's all. I promise." His words just kept plucking at her tightly wound nerves. "Charlotte." Her name on his lips kind of creeped her out, and she fought the urge to shiver.

"You didn't happen to see a necklace around my neck, did you?" Absentmindedly, she put her hand to her throat. "Maybe when you pulled me out? It was round and had a little star on it."

His lips flattened into a thin line and he shook his head. "No. Sorry."

Charlie paused, waiting for her intuition to tell her if he was lying. But everything about this guy seemed off. Everything about him screamed *watch your back*, which made no sense. After all, he had pulled her from the river and saved her from drowning.

"Okay. Well, you can call me Charlie. That's what everyone else does."

"Charlie," he muttered. "I like that."

"So—" Awkward tension crept up between them. "What's your name?"

"Daniel."

"Daniel." Charlie swayed on her feet and jerked her thumb toward the woods. "Well, it's nice to meet you and all, but I'd really like to see if we could make it to the river before the sun sets. The last thing I want is to spend the night in these woods."

"Of course. I'll just pack up my campsite and we'll head that way."

"Uh...okay," Charlie said tentatively. Why did he need to move his campsite?

"I was going to move closer to the water today. Like I said, it's not always easy to keep things straight in these woods, so if we do find your family maybe I'll go with you guys if that's okay. Try to get on the trails a more traditional way."

"Sure," she said. "That would be good. And much safer for you." She glanced around again. These woods were still haunted by at least one ghost, and possibly more, if the girl was to be believed. "What can I do to help?"

CHAPTER 9

Jen stood by the window of Charlie's bedroom and watched as Sergeant Hicks picked through Charlie's things, looking for some sort of clue. Even though she couldn't see the dark halo emanating from him, just knowing it was there made her uneasy, especially as he grabbed a pair of Charlie's panties and onto held them for a few seconds. Jen made a mental note to tell Charlie, just in case she wanted to burn them once they found her.

"She took her phone with her?" he asked.

"Yes," Jen said. She folded her arms across her chest and frowned. "I showed you the text, remember?"

"Right," Hicks said. He moved on.

Jen glanced out the window and watched Lisa lead

two officers and Daphne down the path to the river. She wished they could've all gone together.

"So, is this common? Does your cousin often just wander off?"

"It was a beautiful morning. She's on vacation," Jen said, feeling a little defensive. She bristled. "She took a walk."

"Of course." He smiled, but it never touched his eyes. "It's not uncommon, you know."

"What?" Jen asked.

"For someone to get lost around here. It happens, probably more than it should," Hicks said.

"Why is that?" Jen asked.

"People are curious about the woods here. Because of the legend."

"Sure, something about the Devil's Snare?" Jen asked. "It's a curse, right?"

He nodded. "Right. If you believe in curses."

Jen felt the hair on the back of her neck stand up, and she fought the tremor threatening to shake through her. She did believe in curses. "My cousin Daphne has a book about the place. They hung a witch, right?"

"Yep, they did. Almost three hundred years ago. People always blame her when hikers disappear."

"Who do you blame?"

"Me?" Hicks chuckled. "Well, since she doesn't really exist, I blame the hikers for wandering off the trails."

"Do they ever find them?"

"Sometimes," he said.

Jen swallowed hard. "Alive?"

He opened the nightstand's drawer. It was empty except for a pad of paper and pen with the rental company's logo on it.

Jen pushed, "You didn't answer my question?"

"I didn't," he agreed. "Your cousin sure packed light."

"Yes. That's how she is."

"Hmmm." He glanced over to the window. "Looks like the chief just pulled in." He headed back downstairs, not waiting for her to follow.

She couldn't wait until they were gone so she and Lisa and Daphne could start looking more into this curse. Maybe they'd find something in a local library or newspaper archives. Hicks made his way out to the front porch, where he met the chief.

Lisa and Daphne and the officers appeared on the path and made their way back up to the front porch.

"What did y'all find?" the chief asked the officer standing next to Lisa.

"It looked like something fell into the water. But I can't verify one way or the other that it was their cousin."

The chief nodded as he listened. "All right, then. Let's go." The chief and his officers headed back down to their cars.

"Wait, that's it?" Lisa said, sounding annoyed.

The chief turned and gave Jen a smile that sent a chill skittering across her skin. "Oh, don't you worry, ma'am. We'll be back."

The cousins gathered around Lisa and watched the men climb into their cars and drive off down the steep hill.

Jen sighed. A pang of hopelessness filled her chest. "They're really not going to help us, are they?"

"Nope," Daphne said.

"Looks like it's up to us," Lisa added. "We need to find out if there's a local coven."

"Okay. I'm on it." Daphne pulled her phone from her front pocket and logged onto a website that allowed witches to communicate and connect easily.

"Hicks mentioned a curse. You know, because of the witch that was hanged here." She headed back into the cabin with Lisa and Daphne following.

"One of the officers mentioned it too. Said that hikers sometimes disappear because of her."

"So, he believed in the curse?" Jen asked.

"Hard to tell for sure," Lisa said. "He did ask if we were here to look for the witch."

"Why?" Jen asked. She took a seat on the plaid couch, and Daphne plopped down next to her.

"He said that the curse only affects those hikers who go looking for her." Lisa sat in the brown leather armchair and put one leg on the matching ottoman.

"What else did he say?" Jen set her gaze on her sister.

"Not much. Just that no one ever comes out of the woods if they go looking for the witch." Lisa scrunched her brow and twisted her lips. Jen knew that expression well. Her sister was trying to think through the problem. Break it down. Analyze it. Find the most logical solution. Jen just wasn't sure there was a logical answer for any of this.

"What time did Mama say she'd be here?" Daphne asked.

"She'll be here tonight. Do you want me to text her?" Jen asked.

Daphne looked up from her phone. "It's gonna be dark soon."

"I know," Lisa said. "That's what I'm worried about."

"Maybe we should head to town," Jen said. "Go to the library before they close. Then we can get some dinner. I'll bet you the librarian knows about the witch."

"If she doesn't, maybe she can point us in the right direction," Lisa said.

"There's a small newspaper in town and a historical society," Daphne chimed in, reading from her phone. Her voice sounded hopeful for a moment but her face fell. "Dammit. They're both closed until Monday." Daphne's phone vibrated in her hand. "Okay, Mom's on her way," she said. "She's bringing Jason with her."

"Good," Lisa said.

"Oh. Wow," Daphne said. Jen and Lisa both perked up at the surprise in Daphne's tone.

"What?" Lisa asked.

"Tom's with her too."

"What?" Lisa asked. "How did Tom even get wind of this?"

Jen got up from the couch and headed for the kitchen. She grabbed her purse from the breakfast bar and slung it over her shoulder. "We should get out of here. The streets are gonna roll up on us if we don't."

"Jennifer Lee. What did you do?" Lisa asked using a stern tone.

"What?" Jen frowned. "I texted him, okay?"

"Why?"

"I figured he could help us. And he still cares about Charlie. A lot. So..."

"So, what? You're just leveraging the feelings of a supernatural creature? That's kind of dangerous, don't you think?" Lisa rose from the couch and took her purse hanging from one of the chairs. She slipped it over her head and the small bag rested at her hip.

"It's fine. He knows how she feels about him. I think he just wants to make things right," Jen said.

"Charlie's gonna kill you." Daphne hopped to her feet and gave her cousin a knowing smirk.

"Good. I hope she does," Jen said. "Because that

would mean she was safe and sound with us. Until then, I'm going to do everything in my power to make sure she gets the chance to be mad at me. Now, move it. We're burning daylight."

CHAPTER 10

The pain started in the back of her foot. Dull at first, it grew sharper with each step. Her wet socks weren't helping the situation. Still, Charlie pressed onward trying not to let it slow her down too much. The cool scent of water hung in the air. It had to be close by. She strained her ears, listening for the sound of rapids or waterfalls. Anything that meant they were moving in the right direction.

"You've been limping like that for the last half hour," Daniel said.

"I'm fine. Let's just keep going," she said, ignoring the way he sounded half-concerned and half-irritated. What was his deal?

"We should stop. Make camp. Eat. You've been

through a lot today." He stopped in his tracks and dropped his pack to the ground.

Charlie kept moving forward. Something hard struck her right shoulder blade then thudded to the ground. She turned, half-expecting to find the girl's ghost standing behind her; instead, something silver caught her eye. A wrapper. She bent over and scooped up the energy bar. This one was cookies'n cream-flavored. Her stomach rumbled. "Did you just throw this at me?"

He shrugged.

Charlie rolled her eyes and scowled. She fumbled with it for a second before ripping open the plastic wrapper with her teeth. A sharp pain traveled from her heel up her calf and she finally succumbed. She sat down hard on the ground and gobbled down the chalky energy bar, ignoring the slightly rancid aftertaste. "How much farther do you think we have to go?"

"I don't know." He glanced around. That look of confusion was back on his face, and he didn't offer up more of an explanation. Instead, he fiddled around with the contents of his backpack, moving them back and forth. Finally, he looked up at the sky. "It's getting late."

"We should go, then." She started to get to her feet. "I don't want to be here after dark."

"I told you, you're safe with me," he said. "I won't hurt you."

"I know, it's just my family is probably worried sick."

The words came out too fast and too defensively, making her cringe.

"I'm sure they are, but it's gonna be dark soon. I've some MREs."

"Daniel...I saw something in these woods earlier today. I don't want to run into it tonight. We should keep moving toward the river."

He stared at her blankly for a moment, then dug around in his pack. He pulled out a dingy red pack with a white first-aid cross stitched on the side. "You should let me take a look at that foot. Take off your boot."

"No." She hesitated. "My foot is swollen. If I take it off, I won't be able to get it back on."

"Maybe not. But if you keep walking around on it, it will become infected. Do you really want it to go gangrenous? You could die, or worse," he said.

It was on the tip of her tongue to ask, "What could be worse than dying?" but she didn't. She already knew the answer to that. She had no intention of dying here and haunting these woods for all eternity. They needed to get to the river and the sooner, the better.

"What happens when I can't get my foot back in my boot? Are you planning on carrying me?" she asked.

"If I have to, yes. Will you please just take it off?" He implored her with his dark brown eyes. They reminded her a little of Tom. A pang of longing and rage mixed together made her heart ache.

"You don't understand," she said. "There is something in these woods. Something not happy about my presence here."

"O-kay." He drew out the word and she could almost hear the word 'crazy' emanating from his thoughts. "Do I even want to know what that means?"

"Probably not," she muttered.

"Listen, I know you're spooked. It's definitely been a weird day, but I've been camping here for..." He paused and confusion darkened his face, as if he were trying to recall exactly how long he'd been here, but couldn't. "... weeks. If there was something dangerous here, I would've seen it by now. I mean, I haven't even seen a bear. There have been birds and squirrels and the occasional fox."

Charlie crinkled the silver wrapper in her hand and the sound filled the surrounding space. Shadows played at the corners of her eyes. The trees rustled above her, and underneath it all she could hear something whispering. She listened closely, trying to make out the words, but the sound morphed into a hiss. The skin on her arms broke into goose bumps. The hair on the back of her neck suddenly stood up, and she had the unmistakable feeling that she was being watched. She glanced around expecting to find the spirit girl standing nearby. A crow cawed overhead and but there was no girl. If the spirit was there, she wasn't showing herself. Charlie brought her gaze back to Daniel. "It doesn't matter if you've seen it or not. I have."

"What?" He threw his arms up in the air and shifted his body, clearly agitated by her. By this conversation. "What exactly have you seen?"

A warning bell went off in her head. She did not know this man. Sure, he'd pulled her from the water; he'd seemed nice. But he'd also been...off. Befuddled, and now a little belligerent.

"It doesn't matter." She softened her tone and spoke just above a whisper. It was a trick she'd learned to deal with Scott when he went off on a tirade. She hated that she had to resort to this sort of manipulation. Lisa wouldn't have done it. She would have gone off on the man. But she wasn't Lisa and even though her senses felt stretched thin and hot-wired, she didn't know what he might do if she resisted too much. There were already too many ways for her to die here. She didn't want to add 'at the hands of a strange man' to that list if she could help it. "Fine. We'll camp here tonight."

A slight smile curved his lips and he seemed relieved. "Good. I'll get a fire built and the tent set up." He rose to his feet and tossed the first-aid kit to her. It landed with a rattle, within her reach. "And you can tend to your foot."

"Great," she said, pulling her leg up and unlacing her boot. The coppery odor of blood coated her tongue, reminding her of when she had placed pennies in her mouth as a small child. She choked on the scent as she slid the boot off her heel and found her sock soaked in deep red.

Daniel was unrolling the tent a few feet away.

"How much water do we have?" she asked.

Daniel knelt beside his pack and began to dig through it. His expression became focused. After a minute, he pulled two one-liter bottles of water from his pack. "This is all we have."

Her heart sank to the pit of her belly. "That's not going to last us very long."

"We'll be fine. We'll split a bottle tonight. Drink a little more in the morning and then we'll be found," he said. He offered up a reassuring smile, but it only made her cold. "We'll be fine. I promise."

✻ ✻ ✻

DANIEL PUT ANOTHER PIECE OF WOOD ON THE FIRE AND sparks floated upward before burning out. Charlie stared at Daniel's pale blank face in the orange glow of the flames. He'd put up the tent for her, and, after some back and forth, she'd convinced him to save most of the water for later. The dehydrated MREs stayed in his backpack. He'd offered her another energy bar, but, ignoring the gurgling ache in her stomach, she'd declined, bloated from all the fiber in the two bars she'd already devoured.

When she got home...*if she got home?* a little voice in her head whispered. No. *When* she got home...she would have Jen make her some fried chicken with mashed potatoes and gravy. And a mess of biscuits. And maybe some key lime pie. Her mouth watered, and she pushed the thoughts of her cousin's cooking aside.

She held her breath. The sounds of the night reminded her of some wild place, like a rain forest or jungle filled with singing bugs and howling. Coyotes? Were there even coyotes in these mountains? She didn't know, but if there were, they sounded too close for comfort.

A screeching like no animal she had ever heard before pierced through all the other noises; she sat up straight and peered into the surrounding darkness.

"It's just an owl," Daniel said.

"It wasn't an owl. It sounded like..." *Screaming.* "I don't know what it sounded like, but it didn't sound good."

"You should try to get some sleep." He poked the fire with a long stick, releasing more sparks against the darkness.

Her whole body ached, and her heel throbbed from the blisters that had formed and broken as they walked in circles that day. And she was almost certain that he'd been leading her in circles. She wished she had some of her cousin's quartz stones. Breadcrumbs, Jen called them, because when she set them in place with the right spell, they glowed and showed the way to return. Having them would have at least given her the ability to prove her theory about being led nowhere. It also would have given her cousins a trail to follow.

The real question was, why was Daniel just leading her around? If it continued tomorrow, she would confront him, unless she decided to strike out on her own. The idea of being alone in these woods scared her, but the idea that he might be leading her into some trap scared her even more. She didn't get the sense that Daniel was really evil, though. Just...lost...and hiding something. When she closed her eyes and tried to tune into him, though, all she got was a sort of static.

"Maybe you're right," she said. "You sure you don't mind me taking the tent?"

"No," he said, "not at all. I'll keep watch." His gaze drifted toward the darkness behind her head. A soft *hoo-hoo-hoo-hooooooing* came from a nearby tree, and the image of a barred owl popped into her head. The *hooing* sound continued two more times. Was it looking for its mate? Or was it trying to warn her?

"Great," she said softly. She didn't even have the energy to call up a smile. Slowly, she pushed herself to her feet and limped to the tent. Daniel had spread the sleeping bag out already. Her knees creaked as she bent down and climbed inside, sitting hard. She watched him disappear with the lowering of a zipper. Earlier, when she had cleaned up and bandaged her heel, she had taken off her other boot and sock and left them to dry by the fire. She wished she had thought to at least bring an extra pair of socks in her bag. She made quick work of unlacing the remaining boot and placed it and the sock by the door flap. The need for sleep hit her hard as she crawled over the fleece bag and lay on her side. She pulled half of the sleeping bag over her.

Something hard dug into her hip and she rolled onto her back and sat up. Nothing stood out inside the sleeping bag so she folded it back and ran her hand along the tent floor. Maybe Daniel had set the tent over a rock. Her search came up with nothing. Maybe it was in her coat. She patted down the outer pockets, then the front. Something hard and rectangular met her fingers. She unzipped her coat and shoved her hand into the deep inner pocket. Something cold and metal scraped against her nails. She wrapped her hand around it and pulled out the knife Scott had given her. She'd totally forgotten about it. She reached back into the pocket and dug around a little until she found the compass. Her heart lightened. She didn't need Daniel. She would close her eyes for a few hours and wake up before first light. Then she would take off on her own. Find the river and get home. Once she was safe she would send local law enforcement back to get Daniel. It sounded heartless to her at first, but the small voice in her head kept whispering, *Get away from him.*

And she would, but first, she needed some shut-eye. She rolled over on her side again, snuggled beneath the sleeping bag, and within minutes, sleep reached up and dragged her down into the darkness.

CHAPTER 11

E vangeline wound her way up the mountain, the darkness hanging like a thick curtain. She was a good driver, but her brights didn't penetrate very far. The three of them filled the bench seat of her old truck with Evangeline driving, Tom in the middle, and Jason next to the passenger window. Jason held tight to the safety bar, leaning as far right as he possibly could without too much discomfort. His fingers were a little numb from holding onto the bar so tightly for so long, and sitting next to one of death's minions didn't help, either.

"How much farther do we have to go?" Jason asked. He was ready to be out of this truck.

"Not much longer," Evangeline said. "You could help

me look for this road. From Jen's directions, it's not easy to find."

"Yes, ma'am," Jason said, sitting up a little straighter. "Do you know if it's on the right or the left?"

"Left," Evangeline said.

Jason concentrated on the left side of the road. From the corner of his, eye he could see Tom staring straight ahead wearing a simper on his lips that irritated Jason to no end. He wished, not for the first time, that Evangeline had just said no to Tom's request to come with them.

"It's right up here, Evangeline," Tom said. He pointed into the darkness. "Wait for it. There. Do you see that small reflective circle?"

Jason scowled and saw the red marker just as the headlights hit it. Evangeline flicked on her turn signal and slowed down. She yawned and pulled onto the gravel road. The incline became steep almost immediately and she shifted down into first gear. Slowly they made their way up the hill. From the corner of his eye something moved in the darkness, and Jason caught sight of a doe and a buck moving through the trees.

"There's Daphne's truck," Evangeline said brightly. She pulled in next to Daphne's SUV and set the parking brake. "Finally!" She blew out a sigh of relief. A slight smile curved her lips. "Jason, honey, can you get the bags out of the back, please?"

"Yes, ma'am," Jason said, hopping out. His hiking boots crunched against the gravel, and he reached into the open truck bed, taking his bag and her bag by the handles. Maybe he'd been around them all too long, but the weight of the darkness surrounding them pressed in on him. The cabin glowed against the ominous night. Soft yellow light from the porch and windows beckoned them, offering safety.

Evangeline got out, stretched her arms upward, and curved her upper spine slightly backward. Tom followed Jason out of the passenger side of the truck.

"Anything I can help with?" he asked.

"I got it," Jason said, pushing past Tom toward the front steps. The late evening chill settled around his shoulders. He would need to dig out his jacket if it was going to be this cold. The door opened before he had the chance to knock and Lisa's weary, concerned face was the first he saw.

"Come on in," she said. "We were starting to get a little worried."

"Yeah, well, we had a later start than we anticipated." Jason threw a glance over his shoulder and jerked his head toward Tom coming up the steps carrying two paper bags in his arms.

Lisa's lips twisted into a frown and she gave him a quick nod of understanding. If there was anyone who aligned with his feelings about Tom, it was Lisa, and it secretly made him feel better.

"Oh, y'all are a sight for sore eyes," Jen said as she rose from the navy and green plaid couch. She walked over and hugged Jason's neck. "Thank you for coming."

"Of course." Jason put the bags down and patted Jen on the back.

Tom waited for Evangeline and stood back to let her walk through the door. She carried a black leather tote in one hand and a large paper bag with a handle in the other. Lisa closed the door behind them and locked the deadbolt. Jason noticed as she took a container of salt and poured a line straight across the threshold.

"We were just debating about going to bed or not," Daphne said. She was curled up in a leather armchair with a fleece throw across her lap. She sat up straighter and gave Jason a smile, but didn't get up.

The slight aroma of bacon hung in the air and Jason's stomach rumbled.

"Are y'all hungry?" Jen asked. "I can make y'all a sandwich or maybe fried eggs and bacon?"

"I'm good, baby girl," Evangeline said, putting the paper bag on the breakfast bar and her tote on the floor by her feet. She took a seat on one of the leather bar chairs. "The boys may be hungry though."

"I could eat," Jason piped up. He toed the suitcase nearest his foot. "Where should I put these?"

"There are three bedrooms. Jen and I are sharing," Lisa said. "We figured Evangeline could bunk with Daphne and you guys can either share a room, or one of you can sleep on the pull-out couch. Assuming you even sleep, Tom."

God, he really liked Lisa sometimes. She did not hold back. Jason watched Tom's cautious expression as he glanced from face to face throughout the room. Everyone waited expectantly for an answer. Do reapers sleep?

"I—I won't need a bed," Tom said sheepishly. "Thank you though."

Lisa took a seat on the arm of Daphne's chair and held out a hand. "I win. Pay up."

Daphne rolled her eyes and made a disgusted sound in her throat. "I don't usually carry cash in my pajamas. You'll just have to wait till later."

Jason smirked. "So, what's your plan, then, Tom? You just gonna creep around here all night?"

Tom leveled his gaze on Jason. The corner of his mouth twitched a little. "Actually, I plan to keep watch on the house. Charlie mentioned a spirit. If she shows here, then I'm going to reap her."

"Not before we can interrogate her," Lisa said, rising to her feet, her arms akimbo. She faced Tom.

Tom sniffed, appearing to consider her request. "It will depend on how cooperative she is."

"Will her cooperation help her?" Daphne asked. "You know...determine where her soul ends up?"

"That's not my decision," Tom said. "But we can make her believe it will."

"A little spiritual good cop, bad cop, huh? That's how we're gonna play this thing?" Jason asked, his tone laced with sarcasm.

"It's as good a suggestion as any," Evangeline said, pulling the pins out of the bun at the nape of her neck. She ran her fingers through her silver mane. "Until we encounter her, though, we need to keep looking for Charlie."

"Agreed," Tom said. "So, on that note, I will see you all in the morning." Tom walked to the door, keeping his back to them. He held his hands out, raising his arms to shoulder height, with his hands palm up and his face raised to heaven. An uncomfortable stillness fell over the room as all eyes focused on him. The edges of his body began to soften, like a blurred photograph. Darkness burst from his head and torso, the color of his clothes morphing to black. His black robe flowed around him as if caught in a gentle breeze. A scythe appeared in his right hand. No one breathed until the reaper disappeared through the door.

"Holy crap," Jen finally said, breaking the tension. "That was—"

Lisa finished her sister's sentence. "Terrifying."

"Any way to keep him out?" Jason asked.

"No. Why would we?" Jen asked.

Jason shrugged one shoulder and flashed her a wry smile. "No reason."

CHAPTER 12

A scream pierced the night, and Charlie awoke with a start. When she sat up and glanced around, she found herself in a simple warm bed. Next to her, a boy lay snoring softly, unfazed by the blood-curdling sound. When she looked down at her hands, they were not hers. They were the hands of young man.

This is a dream.

She rose from the bed and peered through the wavy glass of the small window by the bed. It looked out onto a dirt road lined with a few simple buildings. She was dreaming about the past.

A hoard of people marched in the street, carrying torches and dressed in clothes that reminded her of dioramas in museums she'd seen depicting the eighteenth century. They were all men. Some wore gray wigs beneath triangular hats. Some wore brown. Some were old and some were as young as fourteen or fifteen. One man wore all black with white preaching bands attached to his neck, held a rope that was tied around a young woman's neck. She couldn't have been more than sixteen. Charlie's heart beat faster as she watched them drag the struggling girl toward a square. Mud caked her ragged dress and terror streaked her pale, innocent face.

Charlie closed her eyes and took a deep breath to calm her heart. She needed to connect with the boy whose eyes she was seeing through. Within a few seconds, his thoughts pushed to the forefront so she could hear them.

His name was Ezra Fife. He was sixteen and he knew the girl. They attended Reverend Luckett's school together. He'd thought her pretty once, with her jet-black hair and heart-shaped face.

Movement in the front room drew him away from the window, and he slipped on his breeches and grabbed his boots. He crept down the steps, taking care not to wake his younger brother, Thomas, and more importantly, his mother. If she awakened, he would have to deal with the disappointment in her eyes and the sting of her hand on the back of his head for wanting to take part in what she deemed a gruesome ritual.

His father moved quietly through the front room, packing his satchel with his pistol and his prayer book.

"I'm going with you, Father," Ezra said, hopping and tugging on his boot. He tucked the tail of his shirt into his breeches and pulled his suspenders over his shoulders.

"No, Ezra, you are not," his father said. Dark lavender shadows deepened the lines of his father's sun-weathered face. "Go back to bed."

"No, Father," he said. "Someone who knows her should be there to bear witness. To pray for her soul."

His father glanced up. His long face filled with surprise, but it quickly turned to consternation. "And you think that someone should be you?"

"Yes, sir." Ezra nodded.

"You are too young to bear witness to such things, boy. Now, go to bed."

He was forever too young in his father's eyes. "I am almost seventeen, sir. You were married at my age. How were you not too young for marriage, but I am too young to pray for a poor girl?"

His father's mouth twisted into a frown, and he scrubbed his stubbled chin. "You are too impertinent." He sighed and glanced toward the darkened hall leading to the stairs. "Ezra, your mother would skin us both if she found out I let you watch a water test."

"Please, Father, for Abby's sake, let me go."

"Do you know her well?"

"Well enough," Ezra said. "We've gone to school together these last five years." He didn't mention how he'd once thought her a beautiful creature when she smiled.

His father clapped a heavy hand on Ezra's shoulder and squeezed gently. "This is not a game, Ezra. This is a girl's life. What you witness tonight could change you forever."

"I know, Father. But I have faith that God will lead us through the darkness. Don't you?"

His father opened his mouth as if to say something, but then closed it again. He cupped Ezra's cheek, the rough calluses of his palm scraping against his skin. He sighed. "I suppose I cannot protect you forever. Put on your coat."

"What about Mother?"

"We will beg for mercy in the morning."

Ezra grinned and nodded. Excitement wound through his chest and gave his heart a squeeze. It would be the first time he ever saw an accused witch tested. He donned his coat and followed his father to the town square. Ezra bounced on his toes and bit the inside of his cheeks to keep from grinning. If his father believed for one second that Ezra wasn't taking the whole thing seriously, the witch wouldn't be the only one to suffer tonight.

Ezra followed his father into the street and they

joined the tail end of the crowd. Abby stumbled and fell to her knees. Ezra sped up and helped her to her feet. For a second their gazes locked. Her eyes were full of terror.

"Ezra, help me, please." Her voice shook.

"Abby..." he started. The men leading her jerked harder on the rope around her neck, yanking her forward. "I'm sorry."

"Keep moving, girl," Reverend Luckett said.

For a moment, Ezra hesitated. Maybe his father was right. Maybe he was too young.

As if his father had read his mind, he put his hand on Ezra's back and pushed him onward. He gave Ezra a stern look that said, *No going back now.*

The crowd stopped at Garner's stables, and several of the men loaded into the back of a wagon, including the minister and his protégé, William Hicks. They held tight to the rope attached to Abby, making her walk behind them. Those who couldn't fit onto the wagon continued to march alongside it toward the river. Ezra and his father kept a short distance between them and Abby.

They walked along the dusty road that had been cut through the trees and down a steep hill to the edge of the river. As they drew closer, Ezra smelled the cool, clean water.

The wagon stopped and the man got out dragging Abigail forward toward her fate. The men gathered at the riverbank, their torches glowing against the dark forest.

Reverend Luckett and his apprentice Reverend Hicks tracked the girl into the water.

They stopped when the water reached Abby's waist. Each man flanked her, each grabbing hold of an arm. Facing her toward the crowd.

"Abigail Heard," the Reverend began. "You have been accused of practicing witchcraft and killing your master. What say you?"

"I have nothing to say," she answered softly.

Reverend Luckett gave Reverend Hicks a pointed look and nodded. The two men pushed the girl backward and one of them knocked her off balance. They held her under the water for a moment. She struggled and splashed.

Ezra felt sick watching them torture her. After another moment, they yanked her to her feet, holding tightly onto her arms so that she would not fall forward. Her dark hair clung to her skin in spidery tendrils and she coughed.

"Admit you're a witch, Abigail Heard. Repent and you may have God's forgiveness," Reverend Hicks said.

Abby's shoulders shook with tears. "I will not."

"Again," Reverend Luckett said. The two men knocked her off her feet again and held her under the frigid, rushing water. Several moments later, they pulled her up again. She coughed and tried to stand up straight but could not. "Repent Abigail Heard. Repent so at least you won't go to hell when we hang you for witchcraft."

Panic coiled around Ezra's heart, and he stepped closer to the edge of the water. "Repent. Please, Abby."

Abby looked up at him. His breath caught in his throat at the sight of her black, fiery eyes. "I will not."

"Again," Reverend Luckett said. Abby disappeared beneath the surface of the water, this time with no struggle. They held her there for a few moments longer than before. When they tried to pull her body up, they couldn't lift her. Ezra's heart dropped to the pit of his belly. She was dead. The current moved faster and the water became rougher. White crests appeared, curling into waves.

The two men attempted again to raise her still body and move to shore. Reverend Luckett lurched sideways, and he screamed as something jerked him down into the water. Reverend Hicks let go of the girl's body and tried to help his master, but didn't seem to be able to find the man.

"There he is," one of Ezra's neighbors shouted. Several men rushed down river, wading in to retrieve Luckett's lifeless body. The wind picked up around them and the water swelled into a large wave, traveling in the wrong direction. As quickly as they got into the water, the men who weren't dragged under, got out. A banshee scream filled their ears, and Abigail Heard rode the crest of the wave down the center of the river.

"A curse be upon you all and upon this town and this land," she screamed at them, raising her hands to heaven. She began to chant something that Ezra could not quite make out.

"Father." Ezra's heart thudded in his throat, making it hard to breath. He tugged his father away from the crowd, grabbing his hand the way he did when he was a small boy. "Father, please." They stumbled away at first, neither brave enough to look back as the screams of their neighbors and friends echoed into the night.

CHARLIE BOLTED UPRIGHT, CHOKING BACK TEARS. IT WAS just a dream. Or maybe a memory that someone wanted her to see. Perhaps the dead girl she'd encountered had sent it to her. Charlie closed her eyes and pictured the spirit again. She'd worn a dirty nightgown, not a dress. The spirit was not Abby Heard, but something deep inside Charlie, some small intuitive voice told her that the spirit was tied to Abby. The question was how? Had Abby died? Or was she only playing dead before she massacred her captors? Clearly, they'd been right about her. She was a witch. No spirit could have controlled the elements the way Abby had in Charlie's dream.

The smell of meat cooking wafted into the tent and her stomach growled loudly. Pale, filtered light illuminated the forest. She'd overslept. Achy numbness spread through her shoulders, and she massaged her neck to loosen the stiffness. How long had it been since she'd had a real meal? Only twenty-four hours. It seemed like a lifetime ago now.

The crisp spring air chilled the skin of her face, but it wasn't cold enough to see her breath. The dream still clung to her, making her nerves ragged and raw. She knew what she had to do. She had to get away from Daniel, had to get across that river and back to her family.

It was Monday. Ostara. The whole reason she had come. Rebirth from the death of winter. The start of a new chapter in her life. After the initiation ceremony into her coven, she could no longer deny that she was a witch. For the first time, she wished she'd done the ceremony at the winter solstice instead. At least then she might be able to protect herself from the spirit and Daniel.

Charlie scrambled to her knees and unzipped the tent. For a moment, she held her breath and peered out at the fire, which had turned into deep red coals. A makeshift spit held what looked like the carcass of a rabbit or some other small animal, maybe a squirrel? She didn't care; it smelled delicious. She climbed out of the tent scanning for any signs of the dead girl or Daniel. There were none.

She stood up putting her bare feet on the cold
ground. A dull pain spread from her heel past her ankle
to her lower calf. The eerie silence made the hair on the
back of her neck stand up. "Daniel?"

She walked around the empty campsite and found
her socks and her boots drying by the fire. A cold pang
filled her chest. He must have come into the tent in the
night to get the other boot and sock. The blood-soaked
sock had been rinsed and wrung out. The brown-red
stain had faded but had not completely disappeared.
Panic squeezed her belly. Had he used up their two liters
of water to do this?

"Daniel?" she called again, louder this time. The
metal plate of Daniel's camp kit along with a clean metal
spork and the two bottles of water rested on a rock by the
fire. Another energy bar sat inside the plate. Its tan plastic
wrapping looked dull and faded in the early morning
light. A piece of torn paper lay beside it. It read:

Eat and drink. Be back later. ~D

Her stomach agreed and she quickly unscrewed one
of the bottles and drank half of it down in what felt like
one gulp. Then, she took the meat roasting over the coals
and tore half of the little animal's body away. Despite its
leanness, it greased her chin as she stripped each bone of
meat. Even without salt, it tasted delicious.

She left half of the rabbit for Daniel. No need to be
greedy. Daniel had done the work. She let her gaze scan

the woods looking for his tall curly-haired form. He was nowhere to be found, though.

Here's your chance, the little voice inside her head said. *Escape now.* It sounded seductive and ominous all at the same time. Charlie drank down the rest of her water and put the plastic cap back in place. She would take it with her in case she came across a creek or a spring. With any luck, though, she'd find the river.

Daniel's backpack sat next to the pan, unzipped and inviting. He'd put the first-aid kit inside it after she dressed her heel yesterday. She dug through it and found a map, a leather folio, more energy bars and the red bag holding the first-aid supplies. She would just take a few extra bandages and one of the tiny packs of triple-antibiotic cream with her, just in case her heel started to bleed again. The wallet opened as she pulled out the kit. She bit the inside of her lip, debating with herself. Should she look? Was that an invasion of privacy?

Just one look for his full name. *Something to give to the police once you're safe.*

She opened it fully and Daniel's driver's license photo stared back at her. His curly hair was shorter and he looked...happier. Less worried. Less confused.

"Weird," she whispered, and brushed her thumb over the date. The licensed had expired over four years ago. Cold plucked at her heart. How long had he been out here? Based on his supplies, there was no way he'd been lost here for more than four years. She started to close the wallet and the corner of a photo caught her eye. She glanced around. She shouldn't spy on him. She really shouldn't. It was wrong. She would just take a quick peek, then put it back and get the hell out of there. She tugged lightly on the corner of the picture and it slid out of the wallet with ease. The photo was of Daniel and a lovely young woman with long dark hair. They both beamed at the camera. She wore a pale pink T-shirt that had three words printed in a yellow caution sign centered over her belly: Junior-On-Board. Daniel was pointing to the sign. So happy. So carefree. A pang of guilt filled Charlie's chest, and she shoved the photo back into the wallet and the wallet back into the backpack. It was none of her business.

Finally, she took only what she needed from the first-aid kit. She tucked the extra bandages and ointment into the inner pocket of her jacket and zipped it up. Her hand wrapped around Scott's compass. She pulled it out and placed it on the ground next to her. It would lead her to the river.

She quickly put on her dried socks and laced up her boots. Which direction to go? She looked back toward where they had come from, and a chill skittered across her shoulders. Not that way. The brass of the compass cooled her palm when she picked it up, and the site and lid flipped open with the brush of her thumb.

The red-tipped end of the needle floated in the top quarter of the compass face and held steadfastly. She glanced in that direction. North.

Would she find the river if she retraced their steps and found the place he'd first taken her after pulling her out? She reached into the backpack and pulled out the map. It wasn't exactly like the one Scott had used to teach her how to use the compass, but it would have to do. She found north on the map and oriented her compass. The direction of blue curving river cutting its way through the mountains became clear. It wasn't that far. She could find it before afternoon and be back with her family by dinnertime. And then she would send someone for Daniel.

For a few seconds, the lightness in her heart dissipated. By taking his map, she was abandoning him. He was just as lost as she was, wasn't he? Maybe leading her in circles wasn't purposeful. Maybe he just had no sense of direction.

You know better than that, a voice inside her head whispered. *Keep moving forward. It is the only way to survive.*

Charlie closed her eyes and whispered, "I'm sorry, Daniel."

Then she headed toward the river without looking back.

CHAPTER 13

Lisa awoke at 6:00 a.m., more out of habit than anything else. If she were at home, she would have jumped on a treadmill in her condo's gym. She liked to run. It helped clear her head. As she laced up her hiking shoes preparing to search for Charlie, she wished there were a treadmill or clear path that she could run without any sort of complications. The pent-up energy from the stress of the last twenty-four hours made her skin hum. Maybe today's hunt would help expend some of that energy.

Downstairs, she found Evangeline and Jen sitting at the kitchen table drinking coffee. The warm, buttery aroma of biscuits hung in the air.

"Good morning," Evangeline said, putting her coffee cup down on the table. Her long silver hair hung in a braid over one shoulder and the pale pink sweater she wore made her look younger than her fifty-eight years.

"Morning," Lisa said. She headed straight for a cabinet and grabbed a mug and poured hot black coffee into it. She took a sip of the dark bitter roast, letting it wash over her tongue and down her throat, warming her and waking her at the same time. "So, is Jason still sleeping?"

"Yes." Jen leaned forward. "I thought maybe Tom would be back by now, but no sign of him yet."

"How long have y'all been up?"

"Since 4:30," Evangeline said.

"4:30? That's awfully early for vacation," Lisa said.

Dark half-moons punctuated her sister's bright blue eyes. "It's not like we got much sleep anyway."

"Yeah, I can understand that." Lisa grabbed a biscuit from the pan sitting on the stove and a plate from the cupboard next to it. She peeled back the aluminum foil covering a plate of fried eggs and bacon on the counter. She split the biscuit, slid a fried egg and two pieces of bacon between the halves, making a sandwich. "So, what's the plan?"

"Tom has contacts in the area, so I think I'll go with him," Jen said.

Lisa quirked an eyebrow and met her sister's gaze. "Contacts? You talked to Tom?"

"I asked him if he did before I asked him to come."

Lisa considered her sister's words. "So that's why he's really here. Does he even know?"

Jen shook her head and gave her a weary eye roll. "Nope."

Lisa pursed her lips. "We'll have a long talk about means and ends some other time."

"Do we have any leads on whether there's a coven in the area?" Jen rolled her eyes and took a sip of her coffee.

"We passed a gem shop and an herbal remedies shop when we came through town. I thought I'd start there," Evangeline said. "One of the them is bound to have at least one witch working there."

"That's good. I'm sure Jason will want to talk to the local cops. I'll go down to the river again and run a locater spell. Maybe I'll drag Daphne along." Lisa took a bite of her breakfast sandwich. Part of the biscuit crumbled onto the plate.

"What if I want to check out the gem shop?" Jason's voice sounded scratchy and tired as he entered the kitchen, but also full of humor. "Pick up some of those protection crystals y'all carry around in your pocketbooks."

"You're welcome to come with me," Evangeline said, smiling. "There are biscuits on the stove and fried eggs and bacon next to it. Please help yourself."

"Will they even acknowledge they're witches if you

bring a—" Lisa waved her hand toward Jason and chose her words carefully. "A non-believer into their midst?"

"Oh, Jason's not a non-believer, are you, Jace?" Evangeline held out her hand and wiggled her fingers. Jason stepped up and took her hand.

"No, ma'am. I try to keep an open mind these days. You know, in case a dragon pops up and tries to scorch us to death," he said dryly.

"Dragons aren't real," Jen said, teasing. "Now, vampires on the other hand—" she feigned a shiver "—are pretty nasty creatures. You'll want to stay away from them."

"Oh, stop it," Evangeline said. "She's just trying to scare you."

"Right." Jason ran his hand through his hair, giving his head a thorough scratch. "Good to know. Maybe we can also stop by the police station while we're in town, Miss Evangeline."

"Good idea." She gave him a weary smile. "We should also see if they have a library."

"They do," Lisa said before taking the last sip of her coffee. "They were closed yesterday. Maybe you'll have more luck."

A soft knock on the door startled all of them. Jen sucked in a deep breath. No one moved.

"Well, don't everybody get up at once," Lisa said, irritated. She rose from her seat and walked to the front door. Through the decorative stained-glass panes, she saw Tom. He raised a hand to wave. Lisa turned the deadbolt and opened the door.

Tom flashed her a wary smile. He wore clean clothes and looked well rested, but, of course, why wouldn't he? He didn't need sleep and the glamour concealing his true face could be made to look like anything.

"Good morning," he said, his voice full of charm. "May I come in?"

Lisa took a few steps back and opened the door wider, gesturing for him to walk inside. He strode across the room and took up residence behind Jen's barstool.

"Good morning, Tom," Evangeline said. "Are you hungry?"

"No, ma'am. I'm fine. Thank you." He bowed his head slightly.

"What did you find?" Lisa said.

"Something very interesting." He placed his hands on the back of Jen's barstool. "I went down the path and found the river."

"Did you see the place on the bank that I texted you about?" Jen asked.

He nodded. "In fact, I tried to cross the river there."

"You did?" Lisa folded her arms and stood next to him. "What happened?"

"I was thrown back across."

"What do you mean, thrown?" Jason asked.

"Just before I reached the banks of the other side I was physically repelled. I tested the boundary and it stretched for miles along the river, then it cut through the woods for several more miles. I ended up following it in a very large square. Maybe hundreds of acres." Tom drew his lips into a tight frown.

"What kind of boundary can keep out death?" Jen asked, incredulous.

"Hey! I am not death," Tom said. "I reap souls and transport them. I don't kill people."

"I know. I'm sorry," Jen said, her voice full of contrition. "But you are usually immune to magic. Has anyone ever stopped you from doing your job before?"

"No. Never." Tom shook his head. "This definitely felt like magic. Very dark magic."

Lisa blew out a ragged breath. "Well, that's just fan-freakin-tastic, isn't it?"

"It's okay. We're gonna get our heads around this." Jen touched Lisa's arm, trying to comfort her.

"I hope to God you're right," Lisa said. "I just keep thinking about those crows."

"What crows?" Jason asked.

Lisa explained the encounter she and Jen had with the birds the day before. His face became very serious.

"I'll be right back," Jason said. He turned and ran up the stairs, taking them two at the time.

"What's that all about?" Lisa asked.

Jen gave her sister a bewildered look and shrugged. "I have no idea."

"Anyway," Lisa continued, "I was thinking about what you said. Maybe we could turn them. Or..." She paused, knowing that she couldn't take back what she was about to say. Knowing that it would delve outside of the usual realm of their white magic into something grayer.

"Or what, honey?" Evangeline asked.

"No," Jen said flatly. "We're not doing that."

"You haven't even heard me out," Lisa said, using her calmest, most logical voice.

"I don't have to. I can see it on your face." Jen pushed away from the bar and stood up. She put her hands on her hips and pursed her lips.

"Will someone please tell me what's going on?" Evangeline said.

Lisa sighed and opened her mouth to speak, but Jen cut her off. "Lisa wants us to capture a crow and send it across the river to look for Charlie."

"Can you do that?" Tom's expression filled with awe, and he straightened his back.

"The question isn't 'can we,'" Jen said, holding her ground. "The question is 'should we.'"

"You were all for turning one of those crows yesterday," Lisa said.

"It's one thing to take control of an animal that's already been compromised. But it is a wholly different thing to cast a spell on a poor unsuspecting bird." Jen's cheeks flushed with anger.

"Jen's right," Evangeline said, keeping her tone even. "It opens a door. One I'm not willing to walk through yet. Are you?"

Lisa met her aunt's gaze. "I'm fine with it, if it helps us find Charlie."

Evangeline clucked her tongue and shook her head. "Lisa Marie. What's the first rule?"

Lisa sighed and frowned. "Harm none."

"And the second?"

"I don't need a lesson on practicing the craft, Evangeline," Lisa protested.

"What is the second rule?" Evangeline asked, more firmly.

Lisa rolled her eyes. "Govern your thoughts."

"Why?" Evangeline asked.

"Because they are pure energy."

"And?" Evangeline prompted.

Lisa kicked her toe against the empty barstool in front of her. "And we are duty bound to practice without malice."

"I shouldn't have to remind you that you took an oath to do all the good you could in this world," Evangeline said.

"No, ma'am, you shouldn't," Lisa countered, "but we've never faced anything like this before. I don't know if there's enough light between the four of us to drive back this sort of darkness."

"You can't fight darkness with darkness and win, not without losing part of yourself." Jen's gaze held Lisa's. "I would rather fight with light and lose than fight with darkness and win."

Tom shifted his feet. His gaze kept bouncing among the three women. "She's right, you know."

Lisa gave him a side-eyed glance. She scowled. "Shut up, Tom. You wouldn't even be here if we hadn't dabbled in dark magic."

"What?" Tom asked. "What are you talking about?"

"The spell we used to call you that first time," Jen explained, "was not dark magic, exactly. But it was in a gray area. You know, calling death to kill someone."

"I've already told you. I am not death," Tom protested. He rubbed his chin and his forehead furrowed, causing a deep line to appear between his brows. "When you summoned me, it was to retrieve a spirit. An evil spirit, if I recall. You saved lives by calling me."

"Oh." Jen looked confused. "So, if you're summoned by a witch, you won't kill her?"

"No. Of course not. I'm not a barbarian. Every reaper is given a book and there are protocols in place. And if we don't follow the rules, there are consequences."

"Like what?"

"Like..." Tom threw his hands in the air and lowered

his voice. "Complete annihilation. Death is not to be tampered with willy-nilly. Rule number one: Reap only those souls whose names are written in your book."

Jason's heavy footfalls reached the landing above their heads, and they all fell silent as he returned to the breakfast bar.

"Everything all right?" he asked, his voice full of wary surprise as he seemed to notice they were all staring at him.

"Yeah," Lisa said. "Everything's just peachy. Where'd you disappear to?"

Jason patted the gun now strapped to his hip. "I just thought this might come in handy. Especially if birds are gonna be involved."

"I don't understand, honey," Evangeline said.

"I hate birds. They scare the crap out of me. And the thought of a bird being controlled by some evil entity?" He patted his gun. "Well, I like my eyes, thank you very much. So, if a crow swoops down at me, he'll be one sorry bird."

Lisa bit the inside of her lips, trying to contain the grin that wanted to spread across her face. Her eyes met Jen's, though, and she snorted, unable to stop the laughter from bubbling up inside her.

"What?" Jason said. "I'm serious."

Jen and Lisa laughed even harder.

"Don't you pay them any mind. They're just punchy.

You take whatever talisman you need, honey." Evangeline rose from her barstool and patted Jason.

"It's not a talisman, Miss Evangeline. It's a weapon," he explained, his tone wavering between condescending and defensive.

Evangeline's amused expression said she'd dealt with this sort of energy from men her entire life. "What do you think a talisman is?"

"It's...it's for protection, right? To ward off..." Jason fumbled to find the words, "...things, right?"

Evangeline's silver eyebrows went up and her lips curved into a smirk. "You use your gun for protection?"

"Yes, ma'am," Jason said.

"To ward off things, as you say."

Jason opened his mouth to argue, but closed it as if he knew better. He frowned. "Yes, ma'am."

Evangeline cackled softly. "Our protections come in many forms, honey. Some just have more bite than others." She winked at him. "I'm going to wake up my child now. Wouldn't want her to miss out on all the fun."

CHAPTER 14

Charlie's heel ached with every step, and her breath sounded so loud in her ears she thought for sure that Daniel would find her because of it. Every fifty feet, she stopped and looked at the map and her compass, making sure she was still on the right track. What the map didn't show was how steep the incline was the closer she got to the river. She could hear the water in the distance, loud and rushing as it raced around rocks and over cuts in the river where the water cascaded into deep pools that flowed onward toward the ocean.

A chill settled around her shoulders, and she fought against the feeling that someone was watching her. Some part of her kept waiting for him to call her name, but every time she glanced over her shoulder, she found no one there. No ghost. No Daniel. That didn't stop panic from becoming a large pebble lodged in her throat. She kept her eyes on the ground ahead of her, only looking up to grab hold of a tree or sapling to aid in making her way down the uneven terrain. There should've been more noise. Squirrels skittering across tree branches, chattering with each other. Birds singing in the trees above. There was only her breath and the sound of her feet connecting with the thick layer of leaf litter that felt so unstable she thought she could almost sit and slide all the way down the hill.

Dark shadows played at the corners of her eyes and her breath quickened. She paused a moment, looking right and then left, scanning the thick trees for any sign that she was not alone. No one was there. She kept moving.

More shadows danced around her this time, and she stopped and slowly turned her head. She could almost see their dark forms. Were they spirits? Or her imagination? There was no light or translucence to them. If they were spirits, they were like none she had ever seen before. Again, she focused on her feet and putting one foot in front of the other. Dark red mud caked her hiking boots. If she did get out of this alive, she doubted she'd ever get the stain out of the mushroom-colored suede.

An outcropping of dirty white stone caught her attention. She knelt next to it and touched her hand against the cool, jagged surface. Quartz. The energy of it thrummed. She closed her eyes and tried to evaluate if it was magic she felt or just natural energy. There was no spark, just a constant hum that told her it was natural. Quartz could come in handy, especially if she wanted to dispel a spirit or perform a spell. She searched around her for a stick, and when she found one, she used it to dig the smallest of the quartz stones out of the mud. When her stick broke she used her fingers and finally loosened several pieces away from the larger vein. She finished by brushing as much dirt off them as possible and unzipping her jacket. One by one, she dropped all but one of them into the inner pocket of her jacket. The last stone, she slipped into the outer pocket.

The red mud clung to her short nails and stained her cuticles. It reminded her of rusty-colored blood. She wiped her hands on her pants and stood. She did not get three steps before the girl's spirit materialized.

"Conduit," the girl said in her high-pitched voice, "it's time. The mistress is waiting for you."

Charlie's heart jumped into her throat, and she tried to step back but her foot caught on the largest quartz stone jutting from the hillside. No amount of wind-milling her arms allowed Charlie to keep her balance. Gravity won, and she landed hard on her butt. Sharp pain traveled through her tongue and the coppery taste of blood filled her mouth.

Any heat her body had gained from her strenuous descent dissipated, and the sweat on her skin turned icy. The girl glared down at her, and Charlie stared into the spirit's pale, angry face.

"What do you want?" Charlie asked.

The girl tipped her head to the left, and she arched her left eyebrow. Was that a leftover mannerism from when she was alive? Spirits, in her experience, often continued using familiar cadences of speech, facial expressions, and tics, even though they were dead. She once met a spirit with a limp. It was as if they never fully lost being human. Or maybe they just longed for the physical world so much that these things comforted them, reminded them what it was like to be alive.

"What do you want?" Charlie asked again, a little more forcefully this time.

"I want what my mistress wants," the girl finally said. "And she wants you."

A shiver crawled down Charlie's back, but she fought it. She shook her head. "No," she said firmly. "I have to get home." Charlie gulped in air and pushed to her feet. The ghost blocked her from going forward. Charlie lowered her voice, almost growling, "I will push through you, little girl. And trust me, you don't want that."

"Escape is futile. Your fate is hers now."

"My fate?" Charlie said, her voice strident. What she wouldn't give for a God's eye cross at the moment to capture the spirit and get her out of the way. "My fate is waiting for me across that river. And neither you nor your mistress is going to stop me from going home."

"You are home," the girl said.

Charlie's bones ached at the sound of those words. What had Daphne said? People who disappeared into these woods never returned, never to be found?

"Charlie?" Daniel's voice called from behind her.

Charlie closed her eyes and let out a breath. When she reopened her eyes, the girl was gone. And she could hear Daniel lumbering closer and closer.

"Daniel," Charlie said, turning and offering him a conciliatory smile.

"You left me," he said, sounding genuinely hurt.

"We were going in the wrong direction. The river is this way." She pointed down the steep hill. "I found it on your map."

Daniel's expression shifted from hurt to disbelief. "No. It's not."

"Daniel, I have a compass and I know how to read a map." Charlie folded her arms across her chest in defiance.

"It's just...I've been that way before. It seems like it would lead there, but..." He scratched his head. "It doesn't."

"Well, I want to try," Charlie said. "If you don't want to, that's fine. Thank you for all your help. For the food and for..." Her cheeks filled with heat and she looked at her feet, "...for saving me, but I need to find my family."

"No. Everyone leaves me." Daniel's blue eyes sharpened and hardened into little blue jewels. He pulled the knife strapped to his thigh from its sheath and held it out. The blade looked dull, but it could've been just a play of light. "I can't let you leave me too."

Charlie threw up her hands in surrender. Her gaze bounced from the knife to his face. The image of Evan popped into her head. "Daniel, I have an eleven-year-old son who needs me."

"I need you too."

Charlie's stomach turned to an icy rock and dropped deep into her belly. "Daniel, I saw the picture in your wallet. I know you're a father. I know you understand."

His jaw clenched, and he spoke through gritted teeth. "You don't know anything."

Charlie didn't dare break eye contact with him, not until she knew exactly what her next move would be. Her heart beat so hard in her throat she thought for sure he could hear it. "I know that somewhere deep inside you is a nice man. A man who risked his own life to pull me from the water." She took a step backward.

"Stop moving."

"Daniel, you don't want to hurt me. I know you don't. Because if you did, you'd be alone again." Her foot slid back finding a rocky ledge jutting out from the hillside. Dirt and leaves landed below.

"Please stop," Daniel begged. "I don't want to..." His hand shook.

"I know," she whispered, putting another step between them.

"Charlie, I mean it."

"Daniel...I'm sorry. I just...can't." Charlie turned and jumped off the flat, blue granite rock. She landed hard ten feet below and her knees buckled. Gravity kicked in and she lurched forward on all fours, then her legs cartwheeling over her head. She could hear Daniel scream her name. She rolled downhill for what seemed a long time. Rocks and tree roots dug into her shoulders, back and hips, but finally she stopped rolling and slid for several more yards on the slick carpet of leaves covering the forest floor.

She lay there for a moment, breathing hard and staring at the canopy. Bits of gray sky peeked through the tangle of trees. Her whole body ached, and from the heaviness in her side, she was almost sure she'd cracked a rib. Somewhere up the hill, Daniel crashed through the trees after her.

"Get up," she told herself. He called her name again. She gritted her teeth. "Get. Up." She grunted as she got to her feet. The scent of water hit her nostrils and she could taste it, cool and clean, coating her tongue. She threw one more glance over her shoulder looking for Daniel, but there was no sign of him. "Move, dammit," she said aloud, turning to continue down to the river.

* * *

JEN PULLED UP TO THE LOCAL FUNERAL HOME AND PARKED under a tree at the far end of the parking lot. The white clapboard and stone building looked like an old mansion that had been built in the early nineteenth century. She took a deep breath and turned to face Tom, sitting in the seat next to her.

"Are you sure about this?" Jen asked.

Tom gave her a warm, reassuring smile. "If he's masquerading as human, like we do sometimes, then he's in this mortuary."

"And if he's not?"

"That might be a little trickier. I have no doubt that he sensed me as soon as I entered his territory."

"Really?" Jen sat back, her expression full of incredulity. "That's very interesting. Do you sense him?"

"Yes, but not the way you're thinking. It's not like I can triangulate his position like a GPS. I can feel this isn't my territory, and that I'm really not welcome here."

"Wait a minute, this isn't going to cause some sort of... I don't know...reaper fight, is it?"

Tom chuckled. "No, of course not. I wouldn't let it get that far. But he could force me to leave."

"Has that ever happened before?"

Tom glanced at the building. "Only once." He placed his hand on top of hers and gave it a firm pat. "It's going to be all right. Whatever happens, I promise, he won't hurt you."

"I'm not really worried about me, Tom," Jen said.

Tom met her gaze and his warm amber-colored eyes softened. "I'll be fine. It's probably best if you wait here."

Jen took a deep breath and blew it out. She called up a smile. "Fine."

Tom got out and disappeared into the old building. The Chippendale-style portico was flanked by rows of large windows with dark, heavy curtains. In the rearview mirror, she could see the cemetery across the street, its headstones stretching up a steep hill to a mausoleum.

Jen noticed a procession of people filing in to the mausoleum. She watched with some curiosity as the men and women walked in to the building. The mausoleum reminded her vaguely of Greek architecture with marble columns running along the sides. Something dark and shadowy caught her eye, making her bolt upright. She turned and looked directly at it, but it was barely visible. A dark vapor. She didn't have to see it to feel it though. The flesh on her arms broke into goose bumps, and an uneasy dread bloomed inside her chest. The reaper.

She got out of the car and quickly made her way into
the building. Organ music played throughout the grand
foyer. She passed closed double doors on her left with a
sign on an easel that read 'McCune 2 p.m.' under a
photograph of a smiling old man in his eighties with
white hair and false teeth. To her right was an open room
with double doors, no easel, but several coffins of
different colors and different handles. The showroom.
She walked back along the wide corridor that ran down
the middle of the building and found another viewing
room. This one had a coffin in it, as well, but the open
casket was clearly occupied. A shiver ran through her and
she kept moving, searching for offices.

She wanted to call out Tom's name but was afraid of
making too much noise. When all she found were viewing
rooms that were either in use or soon to be in use she turned
around and headed back toward the front of the building.

A door she hadn't noticed before had a simple brass
placard on it that read "Employees Only." She glanced
from right to left and turned the worn brass handle,
pulling it open slightly. She found a staircase leading
down into the bowels of the building. The chemical smell
stung her nose, and an icy chill wrapped around her
heart and gave it a squeeze. This was where the mortician
did his work. Where bodies were drained of their blood
and prepared for the viewing by their family members.

She closed the door and headed out of the building. She'd had just about enough adventure here. It would be better just to wait for Tom outside. When he came back she would tell him what she saw. But her eyes were drawn to the mausoleum. The service must've started, because no more people entered. But the shadowy figure continued to circle the building. Then, without warning, it stopped and turned to look at her. She could feel its glowing red eyes, even from across the street and up the hill. Watching her. Her heart thudded in her throat. She cast her eyes down, not wanting to see the creature anymore. She had no idea of its intentions or if it was friendly, like Tom.

She felt hands on her shoulders and a little choking sound came from her throat.

"It's all right," Tom said softly in her ear. "I see him too."

Relief flooded through her as she realized the reaper wasn't looking at her. It was looking at Tom because it would sense him.

"You should go talk to him," she said.

"Why don't you go with me?" he said, moving around to her side. They stood facing the wall. Neither one of them wanting to turn their back on the creature.

"Why do you want me to go?" she asked.

"You may have questions I won't think to ask."

She turned her head and looked at his profile. "Will it come after me?"

"No," he said. "Protocols, remember?" He didn't offer up a reassuring smile. "However, it will not hesitate to frighten you. It's one of the small pleasures, actually."

Jen frowned and crossed her arms. "Well, that's just great."

"Yes, my brother William is quite fond of it."

"Remind me of that next time your brother orders food from my café."

"He likes your food, and he knows how fond I am of you and your family. He wouldn't dare scare any of you."

She feigned a smile but let sarcasm edge into her voice. "How awesome for us."

"If you're worried, you *can* stay here if you wish," he said. "I do understand." He began to walk away.

A chill settled around her shoulders. She rubbed her hands up and down her arms. The hair on the back of her neck stood up. "Hey, Tom," she shouted. "Wait up!"

CHAPTER 15

L isa emerged from the trail with Daphne
following close behind. A gray mist clung to
the trees, obscuring their tops in some places.
It was as if the sky was falling, and she couldn't tell where
the mist ended and the clouds began. A cold pang filled
her chest.

"Holy shit," Daphne said from behind her. "You think
Charlie's in there?"

Lisa turned to her cousin. She found Daphne
pointing across the river to the woods.

"I don't know, honey." Lisa shrugged. "It's a theory. I
mean we're pretty sure she fell into the river. My hope is
that if she didn't get out on this side, she at least got out
on the other side."

"I don't know if that would be a good thing." Daphne wrapped her arms around her waist and hugged herself.

"Why?" Lisa said. "At least she would be out and alive."

"You really don't see it?" Daphne shifted her gaze from the trees to Lisa. Her expression morphed into incredulity.

"See what?" Lisa stared to the woods. She squinted her eyes trying to see whatever it was Daphne was seeing.

"You know how Tom told you all that there was some sort of border keeping him out?"

"Yeah." Lisa turned her head slowly.

"Well, I can see it. Plain as day. I'm surprised you can't feel it at least. It's giving off an awful chill."

Lisa's gaze bounced from her cousin to the woods. She scanned right and left trying to see something, "I don't see anything, honey. What does it look like?"

"It's black. But not completely solid. Sort of like the aura I saw around the police chief and his sergeant."

Lisa's eyes widened and her heart sped up. "Do you think it's evil?"

Daphne closed her eyes and held out her hands, palms forward, facing the river. "I feel darkness. But not true evil, just all those things that go along with darkness. Fear, anger, longing for something you can't have. It's almost like a heartbeat made up of those things."

"Well, that's not terrifying at all." Sarcasm edged into Lisa voice. "Do you think Charlie's in there?"

Daphne opened her eyes and let her arms drift to her side. "I don't know. Maybe."

"I guess the only way to know is if we try a locator spell."

Daphne nodded. "Let's do it."

The two of them walked along the riverbank until they found the place where Lisa believed Charlie fell. Lisa and Daphne carried their wands in their dominant hands. Lisa unzipped her jacket and pulled a small silver bag from her inner pocket. She loosened the drawstring and placed the bag on the ground in front of them. When opened fully, it flattened into a circle. A pentacle, a star inside a circle was silk-screened on the lining. Daphne unzipped her black leather jacket and pulled five votive candles out. She knelt and placed one on each tip of the star. Then she pulled a green plastic lighter from her pocket and flicked it until the flame appeared. She lit each candle. Then slipped the lighter back into her pocket. She jumped to her feet.

"Okay," Daphne said. "Do your thing."

Lisa pointed her wand at the center of the star and began to make a circle with the tip. She whispered, "Goddess of light, show me through sight, my sister, lost in the night." The flames from the candles grew larger and formed a ring of fire that stretched into a spinning

tube of heat and flames. Instead of opening like a fiery
tornado, the point closed, becoming finger-like. It
expanded over the river, waving back and forth, before
shooting off to the left.

"Now," Lisa said, and continued to circle her wand.
Daphne took off after it, jogging along the riverbank
where she could.

Lisa kept watch over the fire, stealing glances at her
cousin's progress to see its destination.

After a few moments, the fire stopped and hovered
over the center of the water. The closed point opened,
forming a hand that charged into the forest. It hit the
boundary and was forced into the water. The flaming arm
dissipated with a loud hiss and the votive candles blew
out. Lisa's heart sank to the pit of her stomach. Fifty yards
away, Daphne let out a strangled cry.

"What do we do?" Daphne called to her, choking
back tears.

"Come back. We'll do it again. There has to be a way
to make it cross that barrier."

Daphne ignored her cousin and edged closer to the
water. Lisa watched as she stepped into the river, stopping
before the water hit her halfway up her calf. Daphne bent
over and stuck her arm in, apparently digging for
something.

"What are you doing?"

Daphne stood up straight, holding something Lisa

couldn't quite make out in her hand. A few minutes later, Daphne walked toward her, breathless and shivering.

"Look," Daphne said, holding out a necklace with a silver circular pendant. "It's Charlie's."

"We don't know that." Lisa took the pendant and brushed her thumb over the engraved pentacle.

"Yes, we do," Daphne argued. "She was wearing it when we came up on Saturday. I remember seeing it."

Lisa sniffed, refusing to give in to the tears that hovered just beneath the surface. "She's not protected."

Daphne put her arms around Lisa and hugged her tight. "We will find her. Even if we have to cross this river and go get her ourselves."

CHARLIE HELD ON TO SMALL TREES AND SAPLINGS AS SHE descended the steep hill. She ignored the pain in her hips and back. The fall had done a number on her body, and even though adrenaline had kept the pain at bay at first, the closer she got to the river, the more she hurt. She could see flashes of water peeking through the trees, and her chest lightened, filling with hope. How far had she wandered away from the trail leading to the cabin? It didn't matter. All that mattered was getting across that river and out of these woods.

Finally, she reached the riverbank and faced the other

side. She noticed how the trees across the river had buds and new green leaves. As the season progressed, the leaves would fill in and form a thick canopy. The trees on her side were gray, and though some of them had new leaves, most didn't. Most looked nearly dead.

From where she stood, though, the water was wide and deep. The current swirled toward the center of the river. She pulled the map and compass from her pocket. She didn't know whether to go right or left. It wasn't like there was a little red marker pointing to the cabin. What she wouldn't give for her phone. She shoved the compass and map back into her pocket, her fingers grazing over the quartz. She took the stone in her palm and worried her thumb across the top, closing her eyes. She could hear Evangeline's voice in her head, "Tune into the world around you, Charlie. Listen for a heartbeat, And trust your intuition."

Hearing the heartbeat of the world was not always easy but she'd been listening to her intuition her entire life and it rarely steered her wrong. She took the rock and held it in the center of her flattened palm.

"I am a witch," she whispered to herself. "I am in awe of the glory of Mother Goddess and Father God. I am a conduit." It was an affirmation that Evangeline had given her to remind her who she was and what she was capable of. "I am a witch."

She took a deep breath and concentrated her energy

on the rock in her hand. *Show me the way home. Show me the way home. Mother Goddess, I beseech you.*

The rock began to tremble, a tiny quake at first. Charlie held her breath, watching as the stone flipped over. Finally, it leapt off her hand and landed near her left boot. Charlie scanned the bank, heading in that direction. It looked clear. No sign of the spirit or Daniel. She scooped up her quartz and slipped it back inside her pocket and started to walk, ignoring the eyes she felt on the back of her head.

CHAPTER 16

Tom led the way across the street and up the hill with Jen following close behind. She grabbed onto his shirt when they drew closer to the mausoleum. He gave her a look over his shoulder, his face full of calm reassurance, his dark golden eyes said *I will protect you. Do not fear.*

She wanted more than anything to believe him. She understood what it was that drew Charlie to him. His calm assurance. His curiosity. And, of course, those eyes. But something would never let her forget exactly who he was beneath that skin, and she also understood why Charlie had not forgiven him; maybe she never would.

"Tom, I don't know about this. Maybe I should just go sit in the car."

He reached for her hand, taking it in his, pulling her

forward so that she was by his side. "I need you here, and Charlie needs you here."

They headed for the crypt, but it looked more like a house made of stone carved into the hillside. The black painted door was heavy with a large brass knocker that had probably gleamed at one time but now took on shades of green and brown from years of exposure to the elements.

"Wait," she said, stopping on the bottom step that lead up to the door of the crypt, "you want to go in there?"

"Yes," he said. "That's where we'll find the reaper."

"What if he doesn't want to talk to us? What if he's angry that you're in his territory and that you brought me?"

"She," Tom corrected. "And she is very angry that I'm in her territory. But she's also very curious. Let's go in and appease her curiosity. Shall we?" He squeezed her hand and started up the steps. And somehow, she was following him. He gave two quick knocks, glanced around, and then pushed the door open.

Dust and the scent of death lingered in the air. No one had breathed in here for a very long time. A shiver traveled up Jen's arms, settling in her shoulders, and finally her teeth chattered. Tom held firm to her hand and she relished the warmth.

"Ben Azrael," a woman's whisper resounded

throughout the crypt. "You do not belong here. This is not your home."

"No, bat Azrael, it's not," Tom said. "I've only come to help my friends. Show yourself so that we may speak frankly."

"Why do you dress in this human face?"

"It helps in my line of work," Tom said, making no apologies.

"Since when does gathering the dead need a mask?"

"Since I discovered that human spirits are more likely to come to this face, than to yours."

A hissing sound that digressed into a growl scraped along Jen's bones and made her body tremble. She was certain that sound would follow her into her dreams for the rest of her life.

"Show yourself," Tom said firmly.

From the dark corners of the crypt, a shadow slid between the three sets of coffins that lay stacked up on each other lining the east and west walls. The reaper rose up, wearing black robes. The curve of her body left no doubt that she was female. Her face remained in shadow and darkness, featureless except for her eyes. They glittered like bright aquamarines, hard and icy cold.

"What is it you seek, Ben Azrael?" Her voice sounded stronger but gravelly.

"I need to know about the magic surrounding the land the humans call Devil's Snare."

The reaper moved closer faster than any creature Jen had ever encountered. Jen felt the reaper's warm breath on her face. The sickly-sweet scent of mums, roses, and white orchids coated the back of Jen's throat, making her want to gag. Flowers of Death. Underneath the strong aroma was a subtler smell: rot. Like meat left in the sun for too long. Jen's stomach twisted and she covered her mouth.

"Why don't you ask the little witch?" The reaper pushed in closer, and Jen looked anywhere she could but directly into the reaper's face. She completely understood now why Charlie had panicked the first night that Tom appeared and touched her face. It was terrifying to be in the presence of death.

"How would she know?" Tom asked, his tone wary.

"It was one of her kind who conjured it."

"A witch?" Jen asked.

"Yes." The reaper drew out the word, becoming a hiss. "Can you not sense her, as I sense Ben Azrael?"

"No," Jen said. "It doesn't work quite that way with us. We have a book, but it's not very specific about her magic."

"You are a white witch," the reaper said. "She is made of darkness."

"There is another witch," Tom said. "Her cousin. We believe she may be lost in the forest behind the boundary."

"Then she is lost forever." The reaper moved in front of Tom. He did not hesitate to look her in the eye or shrink away from her in any way. "My condolences."

A pebble formed in Jen's throat. She swallowed hard. "Is my cousin in your book?"

"What is her name?" The reaper asked, never taking her eyes off of Tom.

"Charlotte Payne," Jen said.

The reaper grew still for a moment. Even her robes, which seemed to be caught in a perpetual breeze, stopped moving. Finally she stirred again. "No. Her name is not there."

"Then she's alive, right?"

"There is no way to know for sure."

"Why not? Surely, you would sense her death, even if you can't retrieve her soul," Tom said.

"No, her spell leaves me blind. In nearly three hundred years, no soul has escaped."

"What does she do with them?" Tom asked.

"The humans believe she has made a deal with Lucifer."

"As in the devil?" Jen asked. "That Lucifer?"

"There's really very little difference between devils and angels," the reaper said. "Those are human words. Lucifer was once the most loved of us all. But then he grew jealous and prideful. So, God banished him. But I'm sure you know that story."

"Yes," Jen said.

"Did she make a deal with Lucifer?" Tom asked.

The reaper laughed and the sound of it skittered across Jen's skin like tiny electrical charges, causing her arms to twitch. "Lucifer likes the humans. Likes to put on human faces too."

"Answer the question, bat Azrael." Irritation edged into Tom's voice.

"I am not privy to any such deal."

"How do I get into the forest?" Tom asked.

"You do not. I have never been able to cross the barrier. Only the humans can cross, and they never come out."

"How is she so powerful?" Tom asked.

"I do not know. I only know that if I lose a soul to those woods, I will never have a chance to collect it and take it to its rightful place."

"That must be very frustrating," Tom said.

She gestured and shrugged, which surprised Jen. It was such a human move.

"If a witch goes in to the territory of this other witch," Jen piped up. "What happens?"

"I do not know," the reaper said. "Perhaps you should ask the local high priestess."

"So there is a coven?" Jen said.

"Yes," the reaper said. "Just beware, little witch. Even as a magic wielder, you may not be protected from her."

"That's fine. She's not protected either," Jen countered.

The reaper cackled, and Jen thought her ears might start bleeding from the horrible sound. "Indeed, little witch. Indeed."

"Thank you, bat Azrael," Tom said. "This has been very informative."

"Do not think of making this your home, ben Azrael. You will not like the outcome."

"I wouldn't dream of overstaying my welcome." Tom smiled at her.

"See to it that you don't." The reaper turned and disappeared into the shadows. Jen shivered, this time uncontrollably, and Tom led her out of the crypt, back into the light.

CHARLIE WALKED ALONG THE RIVERBANK SCANNING THE other side for any sign of her cousins. A long burning ring shot forward and when she first saw the flames, she thought the trees might be on fire. Once she realized what was happening, she picked up her pace, her slow walk turning into a limping jog. Her cousin had cast a locator spell. Her heart soared. They were looking for her.

She'd studied the spell a few months back, but had

never seen one done. It had seemed too advanced to her, but Lisa was a master at using the spell. She must be nearby. Finally, she spotted Daphne and Lisa on the other side of the bank.

"Daphne! Lisa!" Charlie waved her arms wildly. "I'm over here. Charlie stopped across the river and stared at her younger cousins. The fire, which spun in a long cylinder, hovered above the river. It stopped suddenly, almost directly in front of Charlie, and she moved closer to the river's edge. The flaming cylinder trembled before finally rearing up and plunging into the water. It disappeared in a loud hiss that sent a chill skittering over Charlie's skin.

Daphne stood almost directly across from her now. Charlie waved her arms. "Daphne," she called, but her cousin didn't look in her direction. Instead, Daphne waded into the water. "No! Stop. I'll come to you!" Charlie yelled.

Charlie scanned the water. The current swirled in the center, moving swiftly toward the falls downstream. Charlie's stomach dropped to the pit of her belly, and she trembled, unsure she could go back into that cold water. Daphne stopped when the river was up to her knees. She pushed the sleeve of her jacket up, bent over and plunged her arm into the frigid water. Charlie watched her with curiosity. When Daphne stood back up she held something small and silver in her hands. Charlie's hand floated to her neck, instinctively searching for her missing necklace. Daphne held it up so Lisa could see and the silver glinted in the light.

"Daphne!" Charlie screamed.

Daphne looked across the water, as if she'd finally heard something. She seemed to scan the bank but then turned and headed back to shore, back to Lisa. A few moments later she handed the necklace to Lisa.

Charlie's mind raced. Why didn't Daphne hear her? Or see her? Charlie scanned her side of the riverbank. Her gaze settled on a large granite boulder perched on the edge of the river. She ran toward it, the pain in her body a distant thrum. When she reached, it she climbed on top, waved her arms and screamed her cousins' names again. Daphne pivoted, facing the river again. She put her arm around Lisa's shoulders and they stared directly out across the river.

Why didn't they see her? Charlie closed her eyes. She didn't relish the thought of going back into that frigid water but she had no choice. She would rather drown than stay on this side.

"Conduit," the girl's high-pitched voice came from behind her. Charlie turned her head and the dead girl stood on the rock next to her. Charlie's heart clogged her throat and she took a step away.

"You stay away from me," Charlie said, holding up a finger in warning.

"Conduit, you must come with me. It's time."

"Stop calling me that," Charlie said in her sternest voice. She turned and looked at her cousins. They were talking quietly. What were they saying to each other?

"I'm here!" she screamed again, frantically waving her arms.

Lisa started to turn, heading back to the trail.

"Don't go!" Hot and fierce tears burned Charlie's cheeks. Her cousins were leaving her. She glanced at the spirit then back to the river before her. She took a deep breath, held it, and jumped.

Her skin twitched, anticipating the cold needles of the frigid water. But that sensation never came. Instead a sharp pain in her breastbone and the feeling of sailing backward filled her senses. She landed hard on her back and it forced the breath she held in her lungs to leave her. Charlie lay against the riverbank gasping, trying to catch her breath. The spirit appeared and bent over her. She stared into Charlie's face with black eyes.

"You cannot leave, Conduit. This is your home now."

"No," Charlie said between deep gulping breaths. "No." Charlie jumped to her feet and tried once again to dive into the river. Within a moment, she landed on the riverbank again. She stared into the pale face of the spirit.

"You must accept your fate. You belong with us now."

"No," Charlie said through gritted teeth. She pushed

to her feet again and hopped up on top of the rock. "Lisa! Lisa! I'm over here!"

Lisa stopped at the trail head and turned around, scanning the riverbank. Charlie's heart leapt. Finally, she'd heard her. Charlie waved her arms again and called her cousin's name. She watched as Daphne hooked her arm with Lisa's and they both headed toward the cabin. Panic squeezed Charlie's heart.

"Why can't they hear me?" Charlie turned to the spirit. "What did you do?"

"Why do you think?" the girl said.

"You've done something to these woods."

The spirit laughed. The high tittering sound sparked across Charlie's nerves like little electrical charges, leaving her feeling raw and exposed. "They can't see you because you are like me."

Charlie's ears began to ring and her stomach twisted so tightly she thought she might retch up the rabbit she'd eaten for breakfast. She stared at the girl, breathing harder. "What are you talking about?"

"You know exactly what I'm talking about, Conduit. You died in that river. Just like I did. The sooner you accept it, the easier things will be for you here."

"Shut. Up." Fear and anger swirled in Charlie's chest, bubbling and boiling, intermingling.

"There is no fighting it. There is no fighting the mistress.

"I am not dead." Charlie's voice wavered and doubt crept into her head. "This is all just a dream. A really horrible dream." She shut her eyes tight and when she opened them again, the spirit was beside her.

"You know it's true. In your heart of hearts. No one could have survived that river."

"Is Daniel? Is he dead too?"

The spirit stared at her with unblinking eyes. She didn't answer the question.

Charlie thought back over the last twenty-four hours. Everything felt so real. She didn't feel dead. But then again, how many of the spirits she had encountered admitted they were dead?

The spirit held her hand out. "Come with me, Conduit. It's time for you to meet our mistress."

"And if I say no?" Charlie said.

"There is no saying no."

"You're gonna have to drag me, kicking and screaming." Charlie folded her arms across her chest. The spirit disappeared, and Charlie quickly glanced around trying to look everywhere at once. Something cold brushed across the back of her neck and slowly she turned her head to see the spirit's palm hovering in front of her face. The girl touched the heel of her hand to Charlie's forehead, and before Charlie could protest or strike it away, everything went black.

CHAPTER 17

Jason waited in the truck as Evangeline ran into the post office to make copies of a flyer about Charlie. She returned, carrying a ream of copies in one arm. She started up the old truck, and Jason held onto the safety bar as she pulled into traffic. She drove to the second stoplight and turned sharply into the parking lot for the Brynn Falls gem shop. Evangeline cut the engine to the truck and left one hand on the steering wheel. She stared at the entrance of the building.

"You okay, Miss Evangeline?" Jason asked.

"I'm fine, honey," she said softly. "I just don't have a good feeling about this place."

"Bad juju?" Jason asked.

"Something like that." Evangeline reached for her

purse by Jason's feet. He wiped his palms on the top of his thighs.

"So, how do you want to play this?"

Evangeline flashed him a curious smile. "I'm not sure what you mean."

"I mean for this interrogation. You want to play good witch/bad witch?"

Evangeline laughed. "Why would we do that?"

Jason shrugged one shoulder. "To get information."

"I see. Well, which one are you?"

"I. Uh...I guess I'd play the good witch, since you're the one with the actual magic mojo."

Evangeline rolled her eyes and patted the top of his hand. "Well, here's the thing, honey, they've got a magic mojo too."

Jason pursed his lips. "Oh."

"You're funny. I can see why Charlie likes working with you," she said.

He gave her a bemused look. "Can I ask you a question?"

"Of course," she said.

"Do all witches have a lie detector in their head like you and Charlie do?"

Evangeline shifted her gaze to his face. Her sharp blue eyes glittered. "Well, truly it comes down to what a witch seeks."

"What do you mean?" Jason said.

"Our coven seeks truth. Which is why lies are so easily revealed to us. But some witches like to seek knowledge. Some seek beauty. Some witches seek to do good in the world. Some seek to be one with nature."

"Do all witches seek something good?"

"Oh, sweetie, no. I wish that was the case. There are many things that can be hidden in the heart of a witch. Including darkness."

Jason paused a moment and thought and considered her words. He let his gaze drift back to the building. "Is that what you see here? Darkness?"

Evangeline gazed up at the building. Her hand tightened around her purse straps. "I can see energy, like Daphne does. Auras, I suppose. There is something dark trying to find a way into that building but there's something blocking it. A protection spell, I suspect, or maybe talismans. Whatever it is, it also keeps the energy inside of the building from flowing out. There is a natural ebb and flow to all energy, good and bad. When someone closes off that flow, it can cause a sort of stagnation. That obstruction makes it harder to clear out the bad energy."

"So everything has this aura?"

"Most things, yes."

"Do I have one?" he asked sheepishly.

"Oh, yes." She smiled widely. "You have a wonderful aura."

Jason sighed and smiled. "Do you think we'll get some answers in there?"

"I don't know, honey. I think we will seek the truth and if there are lies, they will reveal themselves." She grabbed a stack of flyers and pushed her purse straps onto her shoulder. "Now, come on. I'm anxious to get back and find out what happened with Lisa and Daphne."

"Yes, ma'am," Jason said.

A TINY BELL TINKLED ABOVE THEIR HEADS AS THEY ENTERED the shop. Jason walked inside with his mouth agape. There were hundreds of bins, all filled with different types of stones and gems lining the walls of the large shop. A large display of different colored polished quartz competed with a display of amethyst geodes in the center of the shop.

Several hand-lettered signs hung on the wall. One offered a day trip to the gem mine where for $45 someone could dig for their own gems. Another sign offered customers the chance to buy different sized buckets of dirt. The buckets ranged anywhere from $25 to $200, and the sign promised gems in every bucket. Jason shook his head. What a scam.

Evangeline walked past the displays and the bins to

the counter at the back of the store. The glass-front case displayed fine cut gems and different jewelry in gold and silver settings. An old-fashioned cash register sat on one end of the counter with a credit card machine next to it.

Evangeline dinged the bell, and Jason sidled up next to her, watching and waiting to take his cues. He kind of wanted to play good witch/bad witch just to see what would happen.

"Coming," a female voice called from the back room. A woman in her mid-forties emerged through a curtain wearing a long black lace tunic over a long black skirt. Her hair had been dyed jet black, but her roots were growing out in a silver line down the center of her head. She wore thick dark eye liner and what looked like a pound of mascara. Jason had no idea how she kept her eyes open with all that weight on her eye lashes.

The woman plastered on a smile. "Good morning." She seemed to almost float across the floor. "How can I help you today?"

Evangeline smiled softly and set the flyers down on the counter. "Two things. First, would it be okay to hang one of these up in your window?" Evangeline handed her one of the flyers and the woman's smile faded.

The woman read the flyer and looked up at Evangeline. "And the second thing?"

"I have a list of things I need and I'm hoping you'll be able to help me with them." Evangeline dug through her purse and pulled out a piece of notepaper that had been folded in half.

"Okay," the woman said. Evangeline handed her the list and the woman scanned it. "I don't carry herbs here. You'll have to go to the apothecary around the corner for those."

"All right." Evangeline nodded. The woman set a heavy gaze on Evangeline, and Jason watched the exchange between the two women with curiosity. He could feel a chill coming from both of them. It reminded him of dogs circling each other before a fight.

The clerk laid the list on the counter and her lips curved into a half-smile. "This is a very interesting list. I assume you need these things because of that flyer?"

"You assume correctly," Evangeline said, her tone sharper than normal.

Jason cleared his throat.

The clerk shifted her gaze to him and narrowed her eyes. "You're a cop."

Jason stood up straighter. He scowled. "How do you know that?"

She shrugged one bony shoulder. "I know a cop when I see one." She turned her attention back to Evangeline, scrutinizing her. "Are you a priestess?"

"I am not. But I am a healer and the leader of my family."

The clerk touched the photo on the flyer. "Is this your daughter?"

"My niece," Evangeline said.

The clerk nodded. "When did she go missing?"

"Sunday morning. She went out for a walk and never came back," Evangeline said. "We tried the local police, but they haven't been very helpful."

"No, I bet they haven't."

"We were hoping that maybe your coven could help us."

"Where did she go missing?" The woman's voice changed, from curious to wary.

"Down near the river, across from those woods they call Devil's Snare." Evangeline kept her eyes steady on the woman.

The clerk sighed, and a frown caused the wrinkles around her mouth to deepen. "I'm sorry, but we can't help you."

"Why not?" Jason put his hands on his hips.

"It's too dangerous. I only know of two people who have ever gone in and come out of those woods alive." She softened her tone. "I hate be harsh, but your niece is probably dead."

"Hey," Jason interrupted, using his most stern cop voice, "what are you? Psychic or something?"

The woman narrowed her eyes and said, "I've been known to be sensitive on occasion."

Evangeline folded her hands and placed them on the counter. She leaned in closer. "What is your name?"

The woman sniffed and offered her hand.

"Ariel Rose."

"I'm Evangeline. I've been known to be sensitive myself, and my niece is still alive. Can you tell me where I might find these two people that survived?"

"I only know how to find one of them."

"Okay," Jason said. He arched his eyebrows. "Where?"

"Well, you can find Mikaela Heard around the corner. She owns the apothecary."

"She's a witch?" Evangeline asked.

"Yeah. A sole practitioner."

"So not a member of your coven?" Evangeline asked.

"No. Mikaela doesn't play well with others. It sort of runs in her family."

Evangeline nodded and her lips curved into a weary smile. "Well, we appreciate your time and the information. I really need to get the things on my list and get back to our cabin."

"Of course. Just give me a minute, and I'll gather these things up for you." Ariel gave Evangeline a smile. Jason didn't like the pity in the woman's eyes. He watched her walk along the bins, taking stones and putting them inside a small brown paper bag. When she finished she handed the bag to Evangeline. "I also sell a nice line of protection charms, if you want to take a look."

"Thank you. I think we're all right," Evangeline said.

"Sure," Ariel said. She punched some numbers into her cash register and Evangeline handed her a credit card. A few minutes later, the credit card printer spit out a receipt, and the woman tore it off and gave it to Evangeline to sign. "Just a friendly warning, I'd be careful of Mikaela."

Evangeline scribbled her name on the receipt and tucked her card back into her wallet. "Why is that?"

"She can be...unpredictable."

"I see." Evangeline nodded. "Well, thank you for your help. You have a nice day."

"You too. Good luck," Ariel said. "And be careful."

"Oh, don't you worry. We will." Evangeline smiled.

CHAPTER 18

J ason stared at the neon sign. He clenched his jaw. "Looks like she sent us on a wild goose chase."

Evangeline arched one eyebrow and patted Jason on the hand. "Never judge a book by its cover, sweetie. Lots of witches have businesses. And not all of them scream *magic here, come on in*. In fact, most don't." She got out of the truck and headed inside and Jason followed after her. The smell of menthol and grilled cheese sandwiches hung in the air. The apothecary was laid out like an old-fashioned drugstore, soda fountain and all. The Formica counter and red leather stools gleamed in the overhead light. A man dressed in a retro white shirt with a red bow tie and wearing a soda jerk's hat was drying soda glasses behind the counter.

Evangeline gave Jason's elbow a gentle pinch. "I'll be right back."

She walked over to the counter and spoke to the soda jerk. He nodded, said something to her and pointed to the back of the store. There were several rows of shelves that filled up the space between the soda counter in the front and the drugstore in the back. Retro signs guided potential buyers to everything from aspirin to bandages to feminine hygiene products. This did not look like a place they would find any of the herbs Evangeline needed.

Evangeline waved Jason forward and she walked with her head held high toward the pharmacist's counter at the back of the store. An old woman stood in front of the counter leaned on an aluminum cane with the four feet covered with tennis balls talking to a young woman in a white coat. The pharmacist nodded appropriately as she listened to the woman's concerns. She'd captured her dark curly hair in a net that hung down the back of her neck hitting her shoulders. Some of the curls had escaped and framed her thin, angular face. Her green eyes were bright with intelligence and she smiled when she spoke to the old woman.

Jason scanned the counter ,noticing the diabetic supplies in the small section devoted to canes, crutches and a folding walker. Above the counter, a sign read Mikaela Heard, Pharm.D. The young woman handed the older woman a paper bag and the old woman hobbled away. The young woman looked up at Jason and Evangeline and smiled. "Next?" Evangeline stepped forward.

"I'm looking for Mikaela Heard," Evangeline said. Jason sidled up next to her. He glanced at the name tag pinned to the woman's white coat.

"Well, you got her," the young woman said. "I'm Mikaela."

"I have a list of things that I need some help with. Do you think you could help me?"

Mikaela's expression became curious. "Well, I can sure try. What's on your list?"

Evangeline reached into her purse and pulled out the list and handed it to Mikaela. The young woman looked over the list, the smile on her face fading.

"Can you help me with these things?" Evangeline asked. Again.

Mikaela gave Evangeline a tight smile. "Possibly. But you have to answer a question first."

Her green eyes scanned the nearby aisles and then she settled her gaze on Evangeline. She leaned forward and lowered her voice. "Who sent you?"

"I am not sure what you mean," Evangeline said.

"Someone would've had to recommend me. Who was that person?"

"The young woman at the gem shop, Ariel, suggested I try here. Do you not carry the herbs I need?"

"Are you working with them?"

Evangeline gave Jason a quick glance.

"Does it matter?" Jason said.

"Possibly," she said.

"Why?" Jason said. "I think you'd be happy to have new customers."

Mikaela frowned and shifted her gaze back to Evangeline. "Some of these are rare. And expensive."

"Yes." Evangeline nodded. "I know. But I need them." Evangeline reached into her purse and pulled out one of the flyers. She laid it on the counter and pushed it toward Mikaela. "My niece has gone missing. The police have been less than helpful."

Mikaela picked up the flyer and looked it over. "Where did she go missing?"

"Near the woods they called Devil's Snare," Evangeline said, her voice almost a whisper. "The other woman we spoke to said you've been in those woods. Said you're only one of two to come out alive, that she knew of."

"Well, she's not wrong." She sighed. "And Ariel told you *I* would help you?"

"Actually, she said you were unpredictable, and that you didn't play well with others," Jason said. "But we're risktakers."

Mikaela chuckled and glanced up front toward the soda counter. She picked up the phone next to the register and dialed a three-digit number. A phone at the front of the store began to ring and the man at the counter picked it up. "Hey, Andy. I'm going to take my break now. I'll be back in an hour."

"Sure, no problem," Andy's voice echoed across the building. "You're the boss."

Mikaela hung up the phone and took a tent sign from beneath the counter with a clock on it. It read: Gone to Lunch. Be back at: 12:30. She set the time to one p.m. and set it on the counter next to the register.

"Come with me," Mikaela said. Jason and Evangeline exchanged a look. He nodded and the two of them headed through the open door behind Mikaela.

THE SHARP SCENT OF MOLD AND DECAYING VEGETABLES permeated the air, and Charlie awoke coughing, trying to get the taste of it out of her mouth. She struggled against the bindings holding her down. The sisal rope wrapped around her waist and tied her arms to her side. She laid on her back breathing in dust and dirt. Above her, tiny stripes let in filtered light. Someone paced back and forth. Dirt sifted down between the cracks, and she blinked hard to keep it from getting into her eyes. How had she gotten here? The last thing she remembered was trying to get her cousins' attention. And the spirit. The spirit telling her she was dead.

Well, there would be no point in tying her up if she was dead. The spirit lied. Of course, she did. Had she read Charlie's thoughts? Or just read her fears? It didn't matter now. The spirit had gotten what she wanted. Charlie gritted her teeth and jerked against the sisal rope tying her wrists.

"When I get hold of you," she whispered mostly to herself. The sound of something rustling in the dark nearby made her stop and hold her breath. Her whole body stiffened as she listened for movement. The soft sound of crying broke her fear. "Hello?"

Someone sniffled and cleared their throat. "Charlie?"

Charlie's heart thudded against her breastbone like a rubber ball bouncing off the wall. "Daniel?"

He crawled along the floor of the space, scooting through the dirt.

"Where are we?" Charlie whispered, but it came out more like a hiss.

"We're in the pit," Daniel said.

"How did we get here?"

"She brought us here."

"Who is she?"

"She's the witch."

"The witch? You mean, the one from the book?"

"What book?"

"It's just a book I read about this place. "

"Right," he said. "One of the legend books. The only problem with those books is they have it all wrong."

"Yeah, no kidding." Sarcasm edged into her tone. "Daniel, how do we get out of here?"

"There's only one way out. And she's walking on it." He pointed to the floorboard above their heads. Charlie cast her gaze upward and could see the partial outline of a trapdoor. "It's sealed tight. Trust me, I have tried to escape before."

"Do you know how long you've been here?"

"Not really. I've lost track of time. And sometimes my memories are very—" He struggled for words. "Fuzzy. Like some days, I can barely remember who I am or where I came from. Some days, I remember everything."

"What sort of day is today? Fuzzy or crystal clear?"

"Things are clear today. But she's angry with me. I suspect things won't remain clear for very long."

"Why is she angry?"

"Because I failed."

"Failed? How?"

"I was supposed to bring you here. But I—" he sighed loudly. "I liked you. You're nice. I didn't want her to hurt you."

"Why would she want to hurt me?"

The chair scraped across the floorboards above them

and then something that sounded like a chain rattling. A square opened above her head and light flooded in. For a second she could see Daniel's dirty, scared face.

"I'm sorry, Charlie," he said. His eyes widened as Charlie floated up from the shallow root cellar.

"Hush," a voice hissed from above.

A force she couldn't see pulled Charlie through the opening and set her down in a wooden chair next to an old stone fireplace. The trap door in the floor slammed shut. A woman in a ratty black dress with black hair turned to face her.

Charlie recognized her face immediately. It was the girl from her dream. Abby Heard. She was no longer a girl, but the only indication that she was a day over twenty-one was the stripe of silver starting at the cowlick on her left side and trailing all the way to the end of the hair. Her solitude had left her pale and drawn but somehow young. Charlie knew that witches could live a long time but none of them were free from the effects of aging.

"I dreamed of you. I...you're Abigail Heard," Charlie said. "They accused you of being a witch."

"Indeed, they did. Luckett." She said the name as if it tasted bitter in her mouth. "Self-righteous, pompous ass."

"You killed them."

"I did what I had to do to endure. They thought

nothing of ending my life all in the name of their god. Why should I give *them* more consideration?"

"I'm sorry they put you through that," Charlie said softly. "But killing them—"

"Hush your mouth. I do not need your pity. Nor a sermon on morality. You are just as much a witch as me, and when it comes to it, we all do what we need to survive."

"No. We don't. Not if it means taking another's life."

"You think yourself better than me?" She circled Charlie, leaned in and stuck her nose next to Charlie's neck. She took a deep breath. "But I could smell your witchy scent as soon as you came close to the river. I've been inside your dreams and I know what you fear."

Charlie shivered and squeezed her eyes shut. "What are you going to do with me?"

"Well, I thought of baking you in a pie," she said, narrowing her dark eyes. "But it's a little late for that."

Charlie looked on in horror, scanning the room for any sign of human remains. A large cleaver lay on top of the table next to a dough bowl, but there was no blood or bone. Only a few herbs tied together and hanging in the window. Her gaze shifted to the over-sized fireplace and the large iron spit. A fire blazed heating the room. Charlie scowled. "Who is the girl? Did you bake her in a pie?"

"Eliza? No. She is devoted to me."

"I'll bet she is," Charlie muttered. "You're keeping her captive. Just like Daniel. Is that your plan for me, too?"

"Eliza is a good girl. She does exactly what I tell her. Unlike the other one." The witch spat at the floor. She eyed Charlie curiously. "I would keep you, if I could. I think once you accepted your place here, we would get on fine."

"No, we wouldn't." Charlie looked over the sparse room. On one side of the cabin was a bed with a frame made of thick tree branches. It had a dirty feather pillow and an old patchwork quilt. Closer to her was a table and another chair. A cast-iron skillet and a Dutch oven sat side by side in the hearth. A long iron poker and a willow broom leaned against the stone fireplace. A small wooden shelf hung on the wall. If it weren't for the modern canned goods and the box of energy bars, Charlie would have thought this place lost in time.

"You must be close to three-hundred years old. You couldn't have stayed here for so long without help."

"The folks in the town are more generous to me now. Bring me what I need."

"And then you what? You screw with their memory? The way you do with Daniel? It's a spell, right?"

"Yes."

"There's a price for certain spells," Charlie said, her voice full of warning. "You know that. Every witch does."

"Ah. But I will not be paying that price for some time to come."

"Why is that?"

The witch walked behind her. Charlie glanced over her shoulder, trying to keep an eye on her. The witch lifted her skirt, exposing a pale, pasty colored leg. She pulled a dagger from the leather sheath strapped to the side of her thigh. The blade gleamed in the light cast by the fire. She moved faster than Charlie anticipated, grabbing Charlie by the hair and pulling her head back. She held the dagger at Charlie's throat. The witch leaned in close and whispered. "Because I have the likes of you to pay for me."

"So, what? A deal with the devil?"

"Oh, no. I am not that foolish. Lucifer would never let me keep the best parts of you."

"What do you mean?" Charlie's voice trembled.

"You are a ripe peach. All that magical ability just bubbling beneath the surface, waiting to be used. I'm tempted to keep you, but I think I will have to be happy with stripping it from you."

"So, you sacrifice a life and you get to keep yours." The words tasted like ash in Charlie's mouth.

"Yes. My name was written in her book nearly three hundred years ago, but I traded another soul and she passed me by, and I will continue to do so."

"You're talking about a reaper." Charlie's stomach twisted into a tight knot.

"Yes. She lets me take whatever power I want from them as long as the soul is intact." The witch grazed the dagger up Charlie's throat. The cold steel barely touched her skin but she sensed its sharpness. "And you, my dear, you have so much power. I cannot believe my luck. The boundary almost broke when you endeavored to leave. If you had persisted you might have gotten away." The witch held her cheek against Charlie's. Hot tears stung Charlie's eyes, blinding her. "And who knows? I may keep you yet. Trade that worthless man's soul instead."

Charlie closed her eyes and gritted her teeth. "If you're gonna trade me, then just go ahead and trade me."

"In due time." The witch pressed her lips to Charlie's cheek. "First, I must claim your magic."

CHAPTER 19

J ason stood shoulder to shoulder with
Evangeline. A sharp, peppery aroma tickled his
nose and he let out a quick sneeze. Evangeline
reached in her purse and offered him a tissue.
He sniffed deeply and waved her away. A year ago, if
someone had told him he'd be following a witch around
looking for herbs to cast a specific spell, he would have
laughed and probably punched them in the face.

Three of walls of the small storeroom were lined with
floor to ceiling shelves that held jars and bottles—some
clear, showing the exact content and some brown,
obscuring the light-sensitive objects inside. A small, black
wooden cabinet in the center of the room was topped
with a large piece of butcher block. There were several
knives of varying sizes along the side of the cabinet, held

in place with a strip of magnet. A small brass scale with various sized weights sat on top of the block.

Mikaela worked quickly, pulling jars from shelves, weighing the amounts listed on Evangeline's list and putting them into small paper bags. Then she wrote on the side of each bag in a black Sharpie the contents and weight. She carefully checked off each item until she got to the last on the list. Mikaela pulled the jangling key ring from the pocket of her khaki pants, thumbed through the keys until she found the right one before unlocking the black wooden cabinet. Mikaela took a large, clear glass jar with a clear glass top and set it on top of the cabinet. Jason's stomach flip-flopped. It was filled with something that looked like tiny blackened bones. Jason's breath became ragged as he watched Mikaela open the jar and measure out a handful of bones with her gloved hand. Evangeline put one arm around his shoulder and gave it a tight squeeze. She leaned in and whispered, "It's all right, honey. They're not human."

"Yes, ma'am," he said, his voice raspy.

"I hope you're not catching a cold," she said.

"I've got something for that." Mikaela looked up at him with her wide, green eyes.

Jason held up a hand and gave Mikaela a tight smile. "No, thanks. I'm fine."

Mikaela shrugged one shoulder. She took the bones

from the scale and slid them into the paper bag. "Okay. That should be everything you need."

"Thank you," Evangeline said, reaching for her coin purse. "How much do I owe you?"

"Two-hundred and thirteen dollars."

Jason whistled. "For herbs and some bones?"

"It's fine, honey," Evangeline said, patting his arm. "It's about what I expected." She unzipped her coin purse, counted out the money, and handed it to Mikaela. "You have no idea how grateful I am for this." She took the bags lined up on the butcher block and placed them inside her purse.

"So, are you honestly going to search for your niece in those woods?" Mikaela tidied up her workstation, putting jars back into their place and locking the bones away in their cabinet.

"We are. We could always use the help of another witch. Any chance we could get you to join us?" Evangeline asked.

"I'm not really sure what good I would do you," Mikaela said.

"Well, just the fact that you've gone in and come out would be very helpful." Evangeline pushed her purse straps up onto her shoulder.

"Well, that's just the thing. I remember going in, but I have no idea how I got out," Mikaela said.

"What do you mean?" Evangeline asked.

"I went camping with a few of my friends at the state park, which is adjacent to those woods, and we went hiking early one morning. Somehow, I got separated from them. I ended up having to spend the night, cold and hungry and scared out of my wits in those woods."

"So, what happened?" Jason asked.

"I fell asleep at the base of a tree. Next thing I knew, I was waking up in my car," Mikaela said. "It was really weird, but everything about those woods is weird."

"Can you tell us why?" Evangeline prompted.

"Well, I knew the legend about the place and knew the land had belonged to my family once upon a time. According to family lore my ancestor, Abigail Heard, was accused of being a witch. Which isn't surprising because, honestly, my family has been practicing witchcraft since the early 1500s."

Evangeline's hand floated to her throat, and she spoke in a soft, strained voice. "They tortured her, didn't they?"

Mikaela's expression became grim and she nodded. "Yes. The history books all say she was found guilty of witchcraft and hung, but—"

Jason leaned in closer to Evangeline. "But what?"

"We have a grimoire going back nearly five hundred years and it...well, it says some crazy stuff about her," Mikaela said.

"What's a grimoire?" Jason asked.

"It's a book of spells and family history that magical

folks keep," Evangeline said. "I'm sorry, Mikaela, go ahead."

"According to the grimoire, she didn't die. But that's ridiculous," Mikaela scoffed, then folded her arms across her chest.

"I've never heard of a witch living that long but I've known witches that have lived almost two hundred years," Evangeline said. "It may not be as crazy as you think, especially if her longevity is tied to dark magic."

"Wait. Two hundred years?" Jason's said, his voice strident. "How is that even possible? I mean that would mean she was alive around the time of the revolution, right?"

"More like the War of 1812," Evangeline said. "It just all depends on the witch. Most witches will have a long life. My grandmother lived to be a hundred and seventeen and died quite unexpectedly."

Jason shook his head in disbelief. "That's amazing. Why was it unexpected?"

"She went flying without her glasses and flew right into a building. Unfortunately, we're not impervious to gravity or blunt objects," Evangeline said matter-of-factly.

"Oh." Jason's eye twitched. He would tuck that information away for some other time. Right now, it was all he could handle knowing that Miss Evangeline was carrying a bag of bones around in her purse.

"Mikaela, I'll be honest. We need another witch for

our circle. Wouldn't you like to know for sure if your family history is true? I'm sensing that it's something you'll always wonder about."

Mikaela bit her lip and looked at her watch. She took a deep breath. "I don't know. It's just a story."

"What if I told you there's a boundary spell around those woods? Maybe on this whole town," Evangeline said.

"How do you know that?"

"We have a friend with us, a reaper. He couldn't penetrate it. Only a living, powerful witch could possibly pull that off."

Mikaela's face blanched. "A reaper? Are you serious?"

"Yes. He's, well, he's special." Evangeline smiled.

"He's something," Jason muttered under his breath. Evangeline elbowed him in the ribs and he let out a soft oof.

"Can I meet him?"

Evangeline brightened. "Of course."

"All right, then, I'm definitely in," Mikaela said.

JEN SPREAD A THIN LAYER OF MAYONNAISE ACROSS THE SLICE of bread in her hand, added four thin pieces of ham, a slice of Swiss and topped it with another piece of bread. She placed the sandwich on the platter in front of her.

She walked over to the stove and gave the pot of tomato soup a quick stir before she started making the next sandwich.

"You need some help with that?" Tom offered.

"No," Jen said. "I'm good. You just keep doing what you're doing."

Tom went back to wrapping yarn around a homemade cross of sticks that he and Jen had gathered from the yard. Several skeins of yarn were spread out on the table in front of him, and Jen had shown him how to wrap the yarn around the four branches to make the God's eye cross.

"I wish Daphne and Lisa would get back," Jen said, putting another sandwich on the platter. "They've been gone for hours now."

"I'm sure they're fine. They're together."

"I know. It's just I don't have a good feeling about this." Jen stirred the soup again. She pulled a clean spoon from the drawer and tasted for seasoning.

"I know," Tom said softly. "But really there's—"

"Listen," Jen interrupted. She held her breath and stood still. The heavy footsteps on the stairs leading to the front porch were too heavy to be Lisa or Daphne.

Through the wavy glass panes, Jen saw the outline of a woman. A woman she didn't know. She heard Jason's voice. The door handle turned.

"Come on in." He stomped his boots on the heavy

rubber mat before stepping over the threshold. He swung
the door open and gestured for the woman to enter
before him. Jen and Tom traded puzzled looks.

"This here is Jen, Charlie's cousin, and that's Tom.
He's..." Jason frowned. "He's nosy."

Tom rolled his eyes and scowled. Evangeline swept
into the room carrying a bag of supplies.

"I'd like you to meet my niece, Jen Holloway, and this
is a good friend of our family, Tom Sharon," Evangeline
said. She put her bag of stones on the granite countertop
of the breakfast bar and began to pull the small bags from
her purse.

Jen put the half-made sandwich down on the platter,
wiped her hands on her jeans and walked across the
room to shake the young woman's hand. "This is Mikaela
Heard. She's agreed to help us."

Jen shook her hand. "Wonderful. Will your coven be
joining us?"

"No," Mikaela said. "Just me."

"Mikaela's been in the woods before and lived to tell
the tale. She has some very interesting things to share,"
Evangeline said.

"That's great." Jen beamed.

"Are Lisa and Daphne not back yet?" Jason glanced
around the living room.

"No, not yet," Jen said, her voice shifting to fretful.

"Should we go look for them?" Jason jerked his thumb at the front door.

Footsteps on the stairs and the sound of Daphne's voice sent a shard of relief through Jen. "Oh, thank God." She walked over to the door and opened it as they stepped up onto the porch. Daphne's lips were blue and she was shivering. "Oh, my God, what happened?" Jen ushered Daphne into the living room.

"She's fine. She went into the river and she just got a little chilled. That's all," Lisa said.

"That's all? Why did she go into the river?" Jen asked.

Daphne stripped off her jacket, sweater and jeans before Jason and Tom could look away. Evangeline grabbed the blanket folded over the leather armchair and wrapped it around her daughter's shoulders. Evangeline walked her over to the fireplace, snapped her fingers and a roaring fire came to life, heating the space. "You stand right here. I'm going to run upstairs and get you some clean clothes." Evangeline scrutinized Daphne from head to toe. "Take off those socks. They look like they're soaked."

"They are," Daphne said through chattering teeth.

Jen went into the kitchen and put a kettle of water on to make some hot tea. Lisa stripped off her jacket and laid Charlie's pendant on the table next to the two finished God's eye crosses that Tom had made. Jen moved into the living room, sidling up next to Tom. She stared down at the pendant and crossed her arms across her chest. "Where did you get that?"

"The river," Lisa said.

"That's Charlie's," Jen said, picking it up and studying it. "I gave this to her."

"May I look at it?" Mikaela asked, stepping up to the table. Jen gave her a halfhearted smile and put the pendant into her outstretched hand.

"Not to be rude but who are you?" Lisa asked.

"I'm Mikaela Heard."

"She's a witch," Tom said. "She's evidently going to help us."

Lisa gave Jen a worried look.

"What?" Jen said.

"There are only five of us. Seven would be more effective."

"So we don't count?" Jason sounded a little hurt.

Lisa sighed and put her hand on Jason's shoulder. "Of course, you count. It's just you're not going to be wielding a wand."

Jason put his hand on the side-arm strapped to his hip. "This is all the wand I need."

Lisa gave him an amused eye roll and shook her head. She moved beside Daphne and put her arm around her shoulders, rubbing up and down her arm. "How you doing?"

"I'm okay," Daphne said, her teeth still chattering.

Evangeline descended the stairs carrying a fresh pair of jeans, socks and a fuzzy sweater. She lifted the throw from Daphne's shoulders and held it up as a makeshift privacy screen. Daphne quickly shimmied her slim hips into the jeans and dove into the sweater. Once she finished putting on clean warm socks, she grabbed the blanket and wrapped it around her shoulders again.

"So," Jason said. "What's the plan?"

"Lunch. Then plan," Jen said. "Lisa, will you get some soup bowls and that box of crackers out of the cabinet?"

"Sure thing," Lisa said.

CHAPTER 20

J ason pulled open one side of his Kevlar vest,
stuck his arm through the hole, slipped it over
his head and fastened the open side. He
adjusted the straps for a snug fit.

"You know that's not going to protect you," Tom said.
"She won't be coming at you with bullets."

"Maybe not," Jason said, patting his chest. "But I
consider this to be one of my talismans. If my gun can be
a talisman, so can my vest."

"Absolutely, honey," Evangeline said. She dried the
last of the lunch dishes and put it back into the cabinet.

"Evangeline's right," Jen said. She looked up from the
dining table as she finished making the last of the God's
eye crosses. "In fact, before we leave, I'll say a blessing
over it. Give you a little extra protection." She picked up

her scissors and snipped the yarn then before tying it into a knot. Daphne, Lisa and Mikaela all stood around the end of the breakfast bar, finishing up the protection bags.

"You know what we really need," Lisa said, "is a way to weaken her, so we can capture her."

"And what do you propose we do with her once we've captured her?" Tom asked.

"There are things we can do in the witch community," Evangeline said. We can call a Regional Council together. They could handle any sort of justice."

"Why couldn't we just hand her over to the authorities?" Jason asked. "I mean, she's killed people, right?"

"Yeah, and exactly how would that go?" Lisa said, her voice edged with sarcasm. "Here, why don't you take this three-hundred-year-old witch who's killed a couple hundred people over the last three hundred years. Yeah, I'm sure they'd totally buy it." Jason scowled, but didn't say anything more. Lisa continued, "Weakening her is our best chance at capturing her, and Evangeline's right, let a witch's council handle it."

"Well, how do we weaken her?" Mikaela asked.

"There are certainly spells we can use. The most effective would include some part of her body though," Jen explained.

"Wait. What?" Jason asked, a little horrified at the

thought of them needing body parts for a spell. Weren't the bones of animals bad enough?

"Oh, don't look at me like that," Jen said. "It means a piece of her hair or a fingernail clipping. Blood is really the best in this sort of spell though. But I don't know how we would get that."

"What about my blood?" Mikaela asked. Daphne, Lisa, and Evangeline all shifted their eyes to her. "She's my ancestor, so according to blood lore, my blood is her blood."

Jen immediately looked to her aunt for confirmation. Evangeline nodded. "Mikaela's right."

"Are you sure about this?" Jen said.

"How much blood do you need?" Jason asked, not afraid to show his disgust.

"Just a couple of drops should do it," Evangeline said. Mikaela nodded. "Yeah. I'm sure."

"All righty, then," Evangeline said. "I need a vile and a bone from one of those protection bags."

"How long will this take?" Jason glanced at the window. "It'll be dark before you know it."

"Not long. I don't want to wait another day. By then, it could be too late. We'll do this one last spell and head over to the state park." The heavy feeling of dread spread throughout the room with Evangeline's words. "Let's get your hand washed, Mikaela. We don't want you to get an infection from a pinprick."

* * *

CHARLIE TASTED BLOOD. THE STICKY LIQUID RAN DOWN HER forehead, blinded her in her right eye, trailed over her lip and down her chin. It was then she knew for certain that she wasn't dead. Ghosts didn't bleed.

Some part of her was thrilled to be alive, but another part of her just wanted the pain to stop. Extracting her magic turned out to be much more difficult than she thought it would be. The witch's frustrations grew with every stripe of blood, every blister and every bruise that did not lead to Charlie releasing just a little bit of magic to her.

The witch hissed at her. "Where are you hiding it?"

"I told you, I barely have any magic in me," Charlie said in a raspy voice. She had no idea how long this had been going on, but from the pain in her wrists, back and breastbone, it was too long.

The witch held her hand over Charlie's forehand, but did not touch her. She dragged it over Charlie's face, keeping a little distance between her palm and Charlie's body. She continued downward past Charlie's neck, stopping in front of her chest. The witch murmured in a language Charlie had never heard before, and Charlie's heart sped up. Charlie's back arched and her whole body stiffened. For a moment, she thought her heart would burst through her chest. The muscles in her shoulder blades trembled and the sharpness of the pain made her believe the witch might have run her through with a red-hot sword. Sweat mixed with the blood on her face and Charlie tasted salt mixed with copper. She screamed and it echoed through her head.

"I can feel it." The witch sighed. "I can feel it calling to me through my skin. Why can't I get to it?"

The witch balled her hand into a fist, and Charlie's body released against the chair. Her head hung forward and she breathed in deep, cleansing breaths. Just like she had when she went into labor with Evan. In through her nose and out through her mouth. She had eventually screamed obscenities at Scott for talking her into a natural childbirth.

She closed her eyes and tears mingled with the sweat and blood on her cheeks. If she could just break these bindings, she would give that witch a dose of her own medicine. She and Daniel could leave this place behind forever.

You doubt too much.

Evangeline's voice floated through her head. Sweet and soothing. Charlie closed her eyes and remembered the day Evangeline was trying to teach her the simplest of spells.

Charlie and Evangeline had sat at the edge of the marsh away from the house so that there was no chance of Uncle Jack discovering them. The back of her T-shirt had been soaked with sweat. She'd held a small piece of milky quartz in her hand and had tried to make it glow the way that her aunt had instructed, but she had failed once again.

"I want you to listen to me very carefully." Evangeline had leaned forward and placed her hands on either side of Charlie's face. She locked her glittering blue eyes on Charlie's, holding her captive. "Everything that you are. Everything that I am. It all begins with our thoughts. Our thoughts are the most powerful thing that we have as witches, as women, as human beings. Our thoughts can rearrange the energy around us."

Evangeline gently took Charlie's hand and pulled open her fingers revealing the pale piece of quartz. Her aunt plucked the stone from her palm, placing it in her own. "Our thoughts can make this crystal glow."

Charlie's eyes shifted from her aunt's beautiful, weathered face to the stone in her hand. It glowed lightly at first, pale gold with the shimmer of pink before becoming brighter and brighter.

"Our thoughts can make the sky answer to us, baby girl." Evangeline closed her eyes and held her face toward the sky. A cloud, dark and thick shifted above them, blocking out the sun. Thunder rumbled, distant at first, and then very directly overhead. It cracked so loudly that Charlie jumped. Evangeline lifted her hands almost in surrender. A fat wet drop struck her aunt's hands and then the ground around them. The sky opened and the rain poured down on them. Evangeline closed her hands making fists and the rain stopped. She opened her eyes and moved her gaze back to her niece's face. It struck Charlie that except for her hands, her aunt had somehow remained dry, almost as if she had directed the rain to fall in a circle around her. Charlie marveled at such magic.

"How do I do this, Evangeline? I am not powerful the way you are."

"And that, my dear sweet love, is why you're not powerful." Evangeline dropped her hands. "It's not because I am and you aren't. It's because you think I *am*. And you think you *aren't*. Do you understand me, baby girl?"

Charlie had nodded dumbly, still not convinced.

"The magic inside you is tied to more than just your blood. It's tied to your soul. It will work when you believe that it will."

"Like faith."

"Sort of. You must see the thing you want to happen in your mind. Believe it. Then command the energy. It will have no choice but to comply. Now try again."

Charlie opened her eyes and she looked at the witch standing in front of her.

Yes. Finally, she understood exactly what Evangeline was trying to tell, her and now she was ready to accept that her thoughts were what made her powerful. The spirit had been right to call her Conduit. Her thoughts were, after all, the conduit to the magic inside her.

Charlie began to chuckle.

"Why do you laugh?" the witch asked, sounding offended.

"Because I just figured out why you can't get to it."

"Tell me."

"My magic is tied to my soul. You'd have to disentangle it and that would damage them both. You couldn't keep your end of the deal and your reaper will come for you."

The witch paced back and forth. She tapped her forehead with her hand, seeming to consider Charlie's words. "I—" the witch began. She stopped and trained a black gaze on Charlie. "I could trade the man instead."

"You can't. You need him to do your dirty work. Just like you need Eliza."

The witch put her hands on the sides of her head and pulled at her hair, making her look crazy. She pulled her wand from her skirt pocket and pointed it at the floor. The trap door opened with a bang. She growled deep in her throat and swiped her wand in the air. Charlie sailed through the opening, chair and all, disappearing into the darkness.

CHAPTER 21

"**J**ason," Jen called. "Please don't get too far ahead of us." Jason aimed the barrel of the weapon in his hand at the ground and headed back toward the group. They had entered the woods with Mikaela showing them the way. They'd been walking for at least a mile now by Jen's calculations.

"Sorry," he said. "I just think it's good that one of us walk ahead a little as a scout. So, we can see what's coming."

Jen's grip tightened on the wand in her hand and she frowned. "I know but the last thing we need is for us to get separated."

"Jen's right," Lisa said. "That's how they get you."

Jen gave her sister a what-the-hell look. Lisa shrugged one shoulder. "I'm being serious. Haven't y'all ever watched a horror movie? The people who get separated from the group are always the ones who die."

Jen gave her sister a sour look. "You are not funny, and you are not helping."

"The only person who's dying today is that witch," Jason said.

"Come on," Jen said. "That's not what we agreed to. It's not who we are."

"Fine," Jason said, sounding a little disappointed.

"I doubt your bullets would do much anyway," Tom added.

"Oh, yeah? And why is that? I thought she was human," Jason said.

"She is," Jen said. "Sort of. I mean, she's not immortal by any means. But there's definitely something going on if she's over three-hundred."

"I agree," Tom said.

"How much farther do you think we need to go?" Jason asked.

Evangeline stopped and looked around. "From the feel of it, we're definitely in her territory. We should probably form our circle here."

"Hopefully, she'll come looking for us. And when she does, we'll be ready," Lisa said.

"I think Jason and I should walk a perimeter," Tom suggested. "Since we really can't partake in the spell craft."

Evangeline looked around. "All right. Just don't go out very far, okay?"

"Yes, ma'am," Tom said, giving her a little salute.

Evangeline set the bag holding the supplies for the spell down by her feet. She pulled out a black tablecloth sized piece of fabric with a pentacle screen printed on it. She took out several items and arranged them in a specific order before putting a small black metal plate in the center of the pentacle. She placed a votive candle in the center of the plate alongside the vial holding Mikaela's blood, and a small blackened bone.

Jen, Lisa, Daphne, and Mikaela joined hands forming a circle around her. Evangeline lit the wick of the candle, stood up, and lifted her face to the sky. "Let us pray."

Jason walked in a circle around the women, his gaze exploring every shadow. His fingers twitched with every snap of the twig and crunch of leaves. He needed to calm down. The last thing he wanted was to accidentally shoot someone that he cared about.

"Pssst."

Jason turned and pointed the gun at Tom. Tom put his arms up in surrender.

"You idiot," Jason said, trying not to interrupt

Evangeline's soft chanting. He lowered his weapon. "You know I could shoot you, right?"

"Yes. You've made it very clear." Tom moved closer. "I have a proposition for you."

"What?" Jason said.

"If their spell is successful, and I have no doubt it will be, you should kill the witch." Tom looked Jason in the eye.

"Jen said—"

"I know what Jen said. But you and I could end this today. Forever."

Jason glanced at the women, considering Tom's words. "What's your proposition?"

"You shoot her through the heart. When she dies, any spell she has over these woods should die with her. I'll transform and reap her. I take her where she's supposed to go. End of story."

"Will she at least go to hell?" Jason asked. Tom stared at him, his face neutral. Jason sighed. "So what? I don't even get the satisfaction of knowing where she went?"

"Sorry," Tom said.

"Fine. But before you take her anywhere, she has to tell us where Charlie is."

"Even if Charlie's dead?" Tom asked.

"Especially if she's dead," Jason said. "The last thing I want is for her to have to be haunting these woods for the rest of eternity. If she's dead, she deserves peace."

Tom nodded. "Agreed."

* * *

JEN SQUEEZED LISA'S HAND. SHE WAS NOT QUITE READY TO close her eyes. Not in this place. The gray gloom weighed her down. Made her uneasy. Shadows played at the corners of her eyes. She heard Tom and Jason talking softly. Mikaela held her other hand.

Lisa dug her nails into the side of Jen's hand. Jen shot her a questioning look and mouthed the word, "Ow."

"Pay attention," Lisa mouthed back.

Jen rolled her eyes and shifted her gaze back to her aunt. A pale blue cloud engulfed them, and silver sparkles of light danced around Evangeline.

In the distance, a screeching pierced the silence of the surrounding woods. Evangeline continued her invocation, ignoring the banshee-like scream drawing closer. Mikaela held onto Jen's hand tightly, her arm trembling. The spell was working.

A dark shadow appeared above them, and Jen let herself peek upward. The motion of the witch on her broom was just a black blur trailed by a red and orange blur.

"Hold fast, girls," Evangeline ordered. She returned to her spell work. The odor of burning leaves and choking smoke surrounded them. Burning their eyes. Blinding them. When she could stand it no more, Jen pulled her hand away from Lisa's and coughed into her elbow.

Two gunshots went off in the smoky haze. Jen turned toward the flash of the muzzle. Her eyes watered with hot tears. Evangeline held her hands out and lifted her eyes toward the sky. She whispered an incantation, and clouds gathered overhead. Thunder rumbled and the sky opened. Rain poured down through the trees pounding so hard Jen thought for sure there would be bruises. The flames hissed in complaint before extinguishing. Finally Jen could fully open her eyes. A perfect charred circle surrounded them. Jen's heart leapt into her throat as she turned three-hundred and sixty degrees.

"Oh, God," she whispered. Jason and Tom were nowhere to be found.

CHAPTER 22

Charlie lay in the dirt feeling sorry for herself. Thankfully, she was no longer bound but it didn't matter. She was going to die. There was no doubt about that anymore. Her whole body ached. If the witch came at her again, she wasn't sure she could fight her off.

"Daniel?" She sat up and glanced around the thick gloom, trying to make out Daniel's form. "Daniel? Where are you?"

The trapdoor opened and a body landed in the pit. A man's voice she recognized cursed in the darkness.

"Tom?" Charlie crawled closer. Her hands found him, warm and real. The sound of his heavy breathing filled the space.

"Charlie?" Tom said, his voice full of relief. "Oh, my God, you're alive."

His arms enveloped her, pulling her close, and for a moment, she forgot what he was and clung to him. Then she remembered, but didn't let go. "What the hell are you doing here?"

He laughed. "We're here to rescue you."

Charlie pulled away, out of his arms and squinted, trying to see his face in the thick gloom. "Well, good job." She sniffed back tears and suppressed a smirk. "Who is we?"

"Jason's here too." His head tilted, looking at the floorboards above them. "And your cousins and aunt. I think."

"What do you mean?"

"We were coming to find you when she attacked us," Tom said.

"What happened to my family?"

"I—" Tom shook his head. "I don't know."

"So why are you wearing this?" She pointed to his chest.

He glanced down at his jacket. "Because it's cold?"

"That's not what I meant and you know it." Her hand found his cheek and cupped it for a second before pulling it away quickly. "Why are you dressed in this...skin?"

Tom made an irritated sound in the back of his throat. He sighed.

"What?" Charlie said.

"I can't take it off," Tom said softly. "There's a boundary around these woods that she's been using to keep the local reaper out. I figured out pretty quickly I couldn't cross as a reaper, but I could in my human form."

"Well, that's interesting, considering she has a deal with him."

"Her," Tom corrected. "What sort of deal?"

Charlie shared how the witch had lived so long and about the spell she'd cast over the town. Tom listened intently as she told him about the spirit of the girl, and how she met Daniel and, finally, how the witch captured her. Lastly, she said, "She wants my magic, and honestly, I don't know if I'm strong enough to keep it from her. We need to get out of here."

The trapdoor opened again. Tom and Charlie scrambled out of the way just in time to avoid being hit by a falling body. He landed with an audible *oofing* and turned over on his back.

"Son of a bitch," he said. He lay there for a minute, breathing heavily.

"Jason?" Charlie clambered across the floor.

The witch stood, staring down at her through the opening, breathing hard. Charlie gazed up at her. Blood from her nose dripped over her lips. She growled and shut the door. Something heavy scraped across the floor and Charlie heard a door slam.

"Yeah, it's me." Jason pulled himself up into a seated position and dug through the pockets of his coat. Within a minute he found what he was looking for. Something made a clicking noise and a bright round light shined on the floorboards above their heads.

Charlie moved to where she could get a better look at Jason. Blood streamed from his forehead across his left eye. "Oh, my gosh," she muttered. "What the hell happened?"

Jason dug out a handkerchief from his pocket and mopped it across his face.

"I'm not—" Jason winced and sucked a breath through his teeth as his fingers found the gash in his scalp. "I don't know exactly."

"She lifted you in the air and dropped you on your head," Tom said dryly.

"Oh, my God. Did you lose consciousness?"

"Yes, he did," Tom said.

"Is there anything you can do?" Charlie directed her question at Tom.

"I have no magic other than this face," Tom said. "I'm sorry."

"Can you disguise other things?" Charlie asked.

"Like what?" Jason asked.

"Glamour is all about perception. That's why it works so well on humans," Tom explained. He shook his head. "Sorry, it doesn't work on objects the same way."

"Well, maybe with the four of us we can get this door open." Charlie ran her hand over the trapdoor.

"Four of us?" Jason scanned the darkness with a wary eye. "Who else is here?"

"Daniel can help." Charlie took the flashlight from Jason's hand and cast the light around the root cellar. "Daniel? You can come out. It's okay, these are my friends."

Something red caught her eye and she moved closer. His backpack. She shined the light on it. It looked dirtier than she remembered. She scanned the spaced beyond the bag, and the light landed on a pair of blue jeans. Blood rushed through her ears and her heart fluttered against her ribs like a pair of caged birds. She moved the light along the jeans to his plaid shirt until landing on the body's mummified face. Salty tears burned the back of her throat. "Daniel?"

A warm hand on her back made Charlie jump and she almost dropped the light. Jason spoke softly, "Charlie?"

"He...he saved me."

"Was he...was he in here with you?" Jason asked.

Charlie sniffled and nodded. "I didn't know he was dead, though."

"I'm sorry," Jason said.

Charlie shined the light on Daniel's body again. A black feather and small bone tied to a leather pouch around his neck caught her attention. She clenched her jaw and shoved the flashlight at Jason. "Hold this." She unzipped her jacket and reached into the inner pocket, unsure if the witch had stripped her of her things. Her finger struck the cold metal of her multi-tool and she pulled it out.

"You have a knife," Tom said.

"Actually, it's more than that." She opened it up to the sharp blade, held her breath and crawled over to Daniel's body. She cut the leather cord holding the pouch and took it from around his neck.

"What is that?" Jason asked.

"I think it's how the witch controlled him," Charlie said. "We need to burn it. But first, we have to get out of here."

"And how do you propose we do that?" Jason asked.

Charlie noticed the pendant around his neck, a silver pentacle that Jen had given him. Hanging next to it was a piece of black tourmaline and clear crystal quartz. She touched the pendant and Jason shivered. "Brute strength and a little magic."

The hinge on the trapdoor just above their heads squealed in protest, but the three of them together, Tom and Jason pushing and Charlie using a simple opening incantation, finally got it to work. Jason could just peer out when on tiptoes and saw the room was empty. Charlie and Tom locked hands for Jason's foot; a quick boost and he was up and out. He quickly reached back into the pit, grabbing Charlie's hand, and then Tom shoved her from below. The protection bag hanging around his neck hit her in the face as Jason grabbed hold of her under her arms and set her down on the edge of the hole in the floor.

She reached out, wrapping her hands around the leather pouch. Her fingers twitched. "Where did you get this?"

"Lisa and Daphne made them. We're all wearing one. Even Johnny Darkly down there."

"I heard that," Tom said in a flat, irritated voice. "A little help, please?"

Charlie and Jason each grabbed one of Tom's arms and pulled him out. Charlie rose to her feet and went to the only door in the cabin. She turned the brass knob but the door wouldn't budge. Jason and Tom came up behind her.

"Dammit," she said.

"Now, what?" Jason asked, looking around warily.

"She's locked us in," Charlie said.

Tom walked over to one of the small windows.

Charlie watched as he ripped down the ragged curtain and wrapped his left hand in it. He reared back his arm and punched out the wavy glass pane. He carefully removed all the small pieces around the edges.

Charlie heard her aunt's soft, sweet voice speaking an incantation. She rushed to the window and saw her aunt and cousins, and a woman she'd never seen before, walking hand in hand toward the cabin.

"Charlie?" Jason said.

Charlie turned her gaze on Jason's panic-stricken face. His chest rose and fell in a heavy pant. The temperature in the room dropped and a chill settled around her shoulders. She blew out a breath in a visible, silvery cloud. "Oh, no."

Jason locked his gaze on her. His hazel eyes widened. "Behind you!"

Something struck Charlie hard on the side of the head and her knees buckled. She blinked away stars dancing before her eyes.

"Charlie!" The heavy iron poker on the hearth sailed across the room and struck the arm Jason held up to protect his head. He screamed and staggered backward, holding his arm to his chest.

Tom offered his hand and Charlie took it, letting him pull her to her feet. Her eyes found the leather bag around Tom's neck.

"I need this," she said.

"Take it," Tom said, quickly slipping it over his head. Charlie opened the bag, her fingers bypassing the crystals, stones and tiny bones for the small linen bag. She opened the drawstring and poured some salt into her palm.

The spirit Eliza appeared in front of the window. "You are not to leave, Conduit."

"We'll see about that." Charlie threw the salt at the spirit. The girl screeched and disappeared. She shoved the linen bag into Tom's hand, grabbed a chair from the table and dragged it beneath the window. "Tom, help Jason."

Tom looked down at the open bag, dumbfounded. "What are you doing?"

"Ending this. Now, help him." She slung one leg over the window ledge, being careful of the shards of glass on the sill.

"Wait." Tom grabbed hold of her hand. "You can't do this alone. I'm coming with you."

"No. I can't lift him. You get Jason out of here before that guard dog of hers comes back."

"And how are you going to end this? You don't have a wand. How are you going to defend yourself?"

"I have these." Charlie showed him the contents of his leather pouch, "I have the spells that Evangeline taught me and I have this." She dug Scott's multi-tool from her pocket and opened the three-inch knife blade. "I can make a wand."

"Are you serious?" Tom gave her a skeptical look.

Charlie glared at him. "Yes. Now, take care of Jason."

CHAPTER 23

Charlie wriggled out of the window and landed on both feet. She scanned her surroundings, getting her bearings and looking for any sign of the witch. The smell of hardwood burning and the sight of smoke sent her heart into overdrive. She heard her aunt's voice reciting an incantation, and Charlie headed toward the sound. A hot wind slapped her in the face as she drew nearer to the corner of the cabin. Every hair on the back of her neck and arms stood at attention.

She peeked around the corner and saw her cousins and aunt holding hands in a spell circle. The witch stood outside them, trying to break through a silver veil between her and the coven. A three-foot-circle of flames burned around them. The flames licked at low hanging branches from the nearby trees. If the fire jumped high enough, this whole forest of mostly dead trees would go up like a tinderbox. Charlie needed to get the coven—*her coven*—to safety. She opened Tom's protection bag and picked through the stones to find exactly what she needed. She'd seen her aunt build many different types of protection bags and, by including stones, salt, bones and herbs, she knew this sort of bag added something extra in case a witch was caught without a wand. And if Charlie knew anything, it was that fighting this witch required a wand.

Charlie plucked out a quartz and a black tourmaline and placed them in the palm of her hand. She took the multi-tool and pressed the handle against the stones in her right hand, then closed her fingers around it. She raised her face to the sky, closed her eyes, and recited a short prayer the way Evangeline had taught her. "So mote it be," she whispered.

With one deep breath, she stepped out into the open.

"Abigail Heard," Charlie said. The knife in her hand began to vibrate. The witch threw a look in her direction, hissing.

The witch raised her wand and swiped it through the air but nothing happened.

"It's working," Evangeline called. Charlie barely heard her over the sound of the crackling thunder of the fire. "Everyone just hold steady."

The wall of flames encircling her coven flared

upward, stroking the branches above her family until
finally the leaves sparked. The fire spread quickly across
the treetops.

Charlie held up her makeshift wand, concentrating
all her energy on the sky above. Storm clouds gathered,
thick and dark, casting a gray gloom over everything. The
first raindrops fell with a dull thud and the flames hissed
in protest, reducing to half their size. The smoke grew
thicker and her cousin Jen dropped her hand, coughing
into her elbow, breaking the circle. The veil dropped.

"No!" Charlie yelled, charging forward. The witch
raised her wand and swiped in an x-pattern in the air.
Charlie flew backward, landing hard against the ground.
Her elbow hit a rock and her hand opened. The stones
and knife scattered across the forest floor. Charlie rolled
onto her side, trying to catch her breath. Hot sparks
skittered across the nerves of her forearm and at a point
in her elbow.

The witch moved toward Charlie. A gleeful leer
stretched her lips. She raised her wand again.

Jason hissed from too close by, "Stay away from her,
you bitch!" His right arm hung out at a strange angle. He
held his weapon in his left hand, aiming it at the witch.

"Jason, no!" Charlie scrambled to her feet.

The sound of his gun firing echoed around them,
bouncing off the trees, reverberating through Charlie's
bones. Time seemed to slow down and she watched the

witch circle the tip of her wand. With a flick of the witch's wrist, the slug changed course, heading toward Charlie. Something hard pushed Charlie sideways. She twisted and landed on her hands and knees. She looked up just in time to see Tom struck by the projectile in the center of his chest. He stumbled backward, his human form dissolving. He turned his dark amber eyes in her direction. If she didn't know any better, she would've thought they were full of pain. A force she couldn't see dragged the reaper up to the sky and he disappeared in a blur.

The witch began to laugh. Charlie stole a quick glance at her family. They'd moved closer, joining hands again. The veil was up again, but Charlie knew it couldn't last. The witch had to be stopped. Charlie focused on the witch's wand. She had to get it away from her. It was the best way to stop her from inflicting anymore damage. According to wand lore, a wand could only be taken from another witch by the spilling of blood.

Another shot rang out, and this time, the witch redirected the bullet back at Jason. It hit him in the leg and he screamed. He fell to the ground, his face red and wracked with pain. He struggled to get his belt off and wrap it around his upper thigh. Blood soaked his jeans. The witch turned her attention back to Charlie.

Charlie searched the leaf-litter for her tool. Her fingers brushed across the black tourmaline first and she scooped it up. When she found the knife, she wrapped her right hand around the cool metal and dragged the blade across her left palm. Warm, sticky blood flowed into her hand, coating the stone.

"You still want my magic? Come and get it, bitch." Charlie chucked the blood-covered stone at the witch as hard as she could. The witch struck at the stone, grazing it. A tiny bit of Charlie's blood smeared across the wood. The wand tip popped and sizzled and the smell of electricity filled the air, reminding Charlie of a burned out appliance. The witch shook the wand in her hand, grunting. Panic molded her pale features.

Charlie charged the witch, throwing her to the ground. The witch screeched, her arms and legs flailing like live wires. Her hand found Charlie's throat where she raked her sharp, dirty nails. Charlie cried out and pressed one hand against her neck, more out of shock than pain. She felt three long welts beneath her fingertips. The witch bucked her hips, throwing Charlie off her. The witch broke off the tip of her wand and pounced, pinning Charlie to the ground. She flattened her body on top of Charlie and shoved the sharp end of her now broken wand at the base of Charlie's chin. Charlie grabbed hold of the witch's wrist with both hands, fighting to keep the sharp stick from piercing her neck.

Charlie inched it away from her throat and the witch bore down harder. Charlie held onto the witch's wrist with one hand, sliding her other hand up to her face. She stuck a finger into the witch's eye. The witch screamed and Charlie twisted the witch's wrist away from her neck and pushed with her hips and legs, rolling them both over until the witch was beneath her. The witch let out an unearthly sound and her eyes widened, followed by a heavy, surprised breath. She stopped struggling. Charlie sat up. What was left of the wand protruded from the witch's chest. Charlie watched in horror as Abigail's hand wrapped around the base, struggling to pull it out of her body. Charlie's stomach lurched and she thought she might be sick. Her hand shook as she reached out and placed it on top of Abigail's. She pried Abigail's fingers away gently.

"Don't. You'll make it worse."

Abigail's eyes became watery and tears leaked down the side of her face into her dark, matted hair. She struggled to breathe.

"Just hang on, Abigail, please." Charlie's chest felt like it had been caught in a vice. Hot tears burned the back of her throat. "Oh, God, this is not what I wanted. I'm so sorry. I...I didn't mean for this to happen."

"I'm afraid," Abigail whispered.

"It's okay." Charlie leaned in closer. Abigail's eyes blinked long and slow. Charlie stroked her hair. She swallowed back the tears threatening to engulf her. This wasn't about her. This was about Abigail. "Don't be scared. It won't hurt. I promise."

"I'm afraid of—" Abby's breath turned to gasps.

"It's okay," Charlie's voice cracked. The image of the terrified girl Abby was the night they dragged her through the street popped into Charlie's head. Underneath everything and despite the last three centuries, Abby was still that girl. Charlie took Abigail's hand in hers and squeezed gently. "You're not alone. I'm here."

Abigail took one last labored breath and her body stilled. The flames surrounding the coven disappeared and an audible whoosh sounded through the trees. Charlie sat back on her haunches and stared down at the lifeless woman.

"Charlie." She wasn't sure who spoke, but her aunt and cousins were at her side within seconds, kneeling next to her. Evangeline slid a warm hand across her back.

"I'm dead," a voice said. Charlie looked up to find Abigail Heard standing at the head of her body. "I'm really dead."

A cold wind blew around them, kicking up leaves. The reaper appeared behind the spirit. Charlie's cousins and aunt dragged her away from the body, terror lined their faces. The reaper's scythe pierced the spirit of Abigail Heard. She screamed but Charlie knew it was from shock and not physical pain. The reaper glanced towards Charlie, its blues eyes glittering. Charlie's breath caught in her throat. That was not Tom.

A howling sound surrounded them and seven reapers appeared. They circled the blue-eyed reaper and the spirit of Abigail Heard.

Charlie clung to her family. "Don't look at them," Evangeline whispered. But Charlie could not look away. She searched the dark hoods of the reapers' until she found what she sought. Tom's dark-amber eyes. He glanced at her for a second before shifting his gaze back to the reaper in the center.

"Bat Azrael, you have been accused of a great crime. The crime of stealing souls that are not written in your book," a gravelly voice said. The sound raked across Charlie's already frayed nerves.

"I —" Bat Azrael stuttered. "May I explain?"

The reapers chanted, "Guilty, guilty, guilty."

Tom took the scythe holding Abigail's spirit and disappeared, leaving the other six to descend on bat Azrael. Finally, when the screams began, Charlie squeezed her eyes closed and put her fingers in her ears to block out the sound.

CHAPTER 24

"A re you sure they said you could go home?" Charlie said, folding the last of Jason's clothes and packing them into his bag. "It's only been a few days. I can't believe they're discharging you already."

"I'm sure," Jason said. "Will you stop touching my stuff?" he scolded and pulled a pair of his boxers out of Charlie's hands.

Charlie laughed. "I was married and I have a son. I've seen lots of men's underwear, trust me."

"Well, you haven't seen mine." His face reddened and he shoved the boxers into his bag and zipped up the top.

She shook her head. Evangeline, Daphne, and Lisa had all gone home the day before, leaving the argument about who would explain to the realtor that the spell the town had been living under was broken unsettled.

Charlie was heading home today, along with Jen, Jason and Tom. It seemed crazy to Charlie that less than a week ago, she'd been running errands to prepare for this trip, and now it was almost over. She'd joined the coven. Just not the way they'd all planned. Thankfully, she would spend the last few days of her vacation at home, where the only witches she had to worry about were the ones in her family.

"Knock, knock," Jen said, walking into the hospital room. "Are y'all ready to go?"

"We are," Charlie said. "We're just waiting on an orderly with a wheelchair. Hospital rules or something like that."

Jen nodded and folded her arms across her chest. Jason took a seat on the edge of the hospital bed and stretched out his leg.

"Does it hurt a lot?" Jen asked.

He shrugged. "A little."

Charlie rolled her eyes. She knew a lie when she heard one. "Well, I'm just glad you're okay."

"Me too." Jason met her gaze. "The real question is, are you okay?"

Charlie looked down at her feet and scraped the toe of her shoe across a dark scuff on the tile. "I will be."

"We'll be back to working cases before you know it. That'll help you get back to normal." Jason smiled.

Charlie gave him a long look but didn't say anything. Jason grabbed her hand and gave it a squeeze. "It was an accident. You know that, right?"

Charlie nodded, afraid to speak. Afraid it would start her crying again. Jen wrapped her arm around Charlie's waist and a sense of calm spread through her body.

"Everything will be better once we get home," Jen said. "You'll see."

Charlie put her arm around Jen's shoulders. "I hope to God you're right."

"Of course I am." Jen smiled up at her. "I'm always right."

* * *

Charlie stopped by the Kitchen Witch Café Sunday morning for breakfast. It was her second favorite part of her regular routine, and for the past three days since arriving home, she clung to her routine to stay sane. Plus, there was something she needed to do.

She was picking Evan up from his dad's at noon and almost stayed in bed. But something had nagged at her, and she found herself sitting at the counter with a freshly poured cup of coffee in front of her, perusing the menu. It was still very early and business wouldn't pick up until after church let out. She took a sip of her coffee, glad to have the place mostly to herself.

There'd been no indication the old man would show. She hadn't felt the presence of someone dead when she entered the restaurant. She looked around, checking every corner for a shadow or a flicker.

Something cold blew across the back of her neck, and she shifted her gaze from the busy café to the old man sitting next to her. He wore the same shirt and sweater she'd seen him in the last time they'd met.

Charlie called up a wide smile for the man. "I was wondering if I'd see you again."

"I still haven't had the fish," he said.

"No, I imagine not," Charlie said, nodding. "You know why no one here is waiting on you, right?"

Pain filled his face and if she hadn't known better, she would have sworn his pale gray eyes had gone glassy with tears. He nodded. "I think I do."

"Is there anything I can do for you? Maybe send a message to someone?"

He folded his hands and stared at them, his face becoming pensive. "You'd do that for me?"

"It's sort of my specialty," Charlie said. "I help people in your situation all the time."

The man nodded and cleared his throat. "Well, I

suppose the thing I need to share the most is that my wife didn't mean it."

"Didn't mean what?"

"You see, after Eleanor passed, I didn't feel like doing much of anything. Not even talking to my daughter. And I should have talked to her. Should've told her things."

"I know," Charlie said, nodding. "It's hard though. So this was about your wife?"

"Oh, yes." He touched a finger to his forehead. "I guess, even old dead guys forget stuff."

Charlie chuckled. "What would you like me to tell your daughter about your wife?"

"Well, as much as I love my wife, she could be a spiteful old bitch."

Charlie bit her lips together to keep her mouth from gaping open. She nodded.

"A few months before she died, she and my daughter had a falling out over the man that April had fallen in love with. My wife swore my daughter would never wear her pearls or her diamond ring, especially not for her wedding. But after Colleen died, I thought that was wrong. April should have those things. If for no other reason than to spite her mother."

"All right." Charlie said, fighting to hold in the laughter threatening to burst out of her. "Did your wife put them someplace? Or maybe you did?"

"My wife put them into a safe deposit box at Bel-com. Box number 4636."

"Is there a key?"

"Yes. It's taped to the underside of the top desk drawer in my study. It was still there when I looked the other day, but April's been talking about getting rid of it because she wants to sell the house."

"I understand. I will let her know where the key is and the number of the box. Is there anything else?"

The old man smiled. "What's your name?"

"My name is Charlie Payne."

"It's very nice to meet you, Charlie Payne. My name is Marlon Forbes. Thank you for this." He gave her the address to April's house. "Just let her know that her daddy loves her. And that no matter what, he's proud of her."

"I will let her know." Charlie smiled wide. "Do you think you can move on now? Or do you think you might need a little help? I have a friend. He's a guide for people like you."

Marlon cast his eyes skyward and a slight smile curved his lips. "Oh, no. I think I can find my way."

"All right, Marlon. You go ahead, then. And if you run into a woman named Bunny Payne, tell her Charlie said hey."

"I sure will," Marlon said, then disappeared.

Charlie pulled her new phone from her purse and

quickly jotted down the information that Marlon had given her. She would stop by on her way to pick up Evan. A smile stretched her lips. This was her life. Her crazy, busy, ghost-helping life, and she loved every minute of it. She took another sip of her coffee and played with her silverware until Jen brought her a plate of pancakes.

AUTHOR'S NOTE

Thank you for reading. If you loved this book and want the next adventure, you can download the next book in the series The Witch's Ladder.

If you love Charlie and want to go along on her ghostly adventures, please join my readers list: http://eepurl.com/czMPgı

By signing up you'll get a free deleted scene from this book and you'll be the first to know about major updates and new releases.

If you enjoyed this book, please give it a rating on Amazon. Your kind words and encouragement can make an author's day (ask me how I know – smile). Of course, I'll keep writing whether you give me an Outstanding review or not, but it might get done faster with your cheerleading (smile).

Want to comment on your favorite scene? Or make suggestions for a funny ghostly encounter for Charlie? Or tell me what sort of magic you'd like to see Jen, Daphne and Lisa perform? Or take part in naming the killers/ghosts for my future books? Come tell me on Facebook.

Facebook:
https://www.facebook.com/wendywangauthor or let's talk about our favorite books in my readers group on Facebook;

Readers Group:
https://www.facebook.com/groups/1287348628022940/ ; or you can always drop me an email,

Email:
http://www.wendywangbooks.com/contact.html

Thank you again for reading!

Check out my other books:

Witches of Palmetto Point Series (Supernatural Suspense)
Book 1: Haunting Charlie
Book 2: Wayward Spirits
Book 3: Devil's Snare
Book 4: The Witch's Ladder
Book 5: The Harbinger
Book 6: Shadow Child (Coming January 2019)

The Book of Kaels Series (Fantasy)
Book 1: The Last Queen

Book 2: The Wood Kael
Book 3: The Metal Kael
Book 4: The Fire Kael
Book of Kaels Box Set: Books 1 -4
Short Stories: Love Lacey

Printed in Great Britain
by Amazon

26811292R00169